LUKE
WARM

LUKE WARM

JACK WOLSKI

LIBERTY HILL PUBLISHING

Liberty Hill Publishing
2301 Lucien Way #415
Maitland, FL 32751
407.339.4217
www.libertyhillpublishing.com

© 2021 by Jack Wolski

All rights reserved solely by the author. The author guarantees all contents are original and do not infringe upon the legal rights of any other person or work. No part of this book may be reproduced in any form without the permission of the author. The views expressed in this book are not necessarily those of the publisher.

Due to the changing nature of the Internet, if there are any web addresses, links, or URLs included in this manuscript, these may have been altered and may no longer be accessible. The views and opinions shared in this book belong solely to the author and do not necessarily reflect those of the publisher. The publisher, therefore, disclaims responsibility for the views or opinions expressed within the work.

Paperback ISBN-13: 978-1-66282-769-3
Ebook ISBN-13: 978-1-66282-770-9

Chapter 1

A Mediocre Individual

The plane touched down under the dreary backdrop of typical German winter weather. Luke, a young espionage agent fresh out of training, stepped from the terminal into the gloomy extremes of what he hoped would be a long stay and a successful career. Dressed in his new wardrobe of a dark blue suit, dragging two ugly yellow suitcases behind him, he looked about the crowd in hopes of spotting his new coworker who was supposed to pick him up.

The long trip from JFK International to Berlin had left him a bit disheveled, and he wanted nothing more than to get acquainted with a shower and bed. He anxiously wanted to get to work but also knew he needed some downtime to unwind from the trip. A certain *je ne sais quoi* filled his dizzy head and ringing ears; it was the first time he had undertaken such a drastic change in his life, and he didn't quite know what to expect next. He imagined this was the feeling President Reagan had experienced three years prior when he first took office: the pride of completing a difficult task, one which seemed insurmountable at times; the new challenges that lay ahead; the difficult decisions that may be made; and what the future would mean based on those decisions.

"Luke! It's good to finally meet you," said a man across the velvet ropes that separated passengers from loved ones. "Your reputation precedes you. Let's hope you're as good in real life as you were in training. My name is John. Welcome to West Berlin."

John was plain by all accounts, not quite the usual portly look of an American middle-aged man. He wore a European suit, not Italian, but probably pumped out from a factory in Germany or Austria. For someone in his early forties, he looked like he exercised regularly; John appeared athletic but not muscular. He was what was referred to in the business as the "gray man." John could walk into a room, not make waves but be seen, and he was forgotten as soon as he left. John was the same height as Luke but made him look like a schoolboy by comparison. Luke had a smaller frame and a baby face. John was a bit more filled out and had light wrinkles around his eyes and forehead. Luke's hands were long, wiry, and smooth, yet lacking a manicure. John's hands looked like they were no stranger to manual labor, but his fingernails were clean and trimmed. For anyone who watched, the scene looked like a divorced dad picking his son up at the airport for their court-ordered "together time."

Luke was highly regarded by his instructors as a natural counterespionage agent. Although he was young, a recent college graduate with a master's degree and no experience in the field, he was a fast learner who constantly exceeded course standards. He was young but had an old soul that helped him win over the aging instructors. He had few, if any, workplace enemies due to his affable personality. This attribute, coupled with his inexperience and thirst for knowledge, made his superiors and teachers take Luke under their wing. Even with this exposure to all his professors and instructors, he was not viewed by the rest of his peers as a teacher's pet. While he was regarded as bright, he also possessed humility, which allowed others to look up to him rather than resent him.

But this wasn't the schoolhouse anymore. Luke was now working for a quasi-military department. Officially it fell under the Department of Defense, but in reality, their efforts fed into reporting for the vice president directly. While other Americans think of the Central Intelligence Agency for the United States's intelligence efforts, there were many others fighting the Cold War. It was an all-hands effort requiring many people. Some organizations, like this one, would rarely be spoken of. Each of the Company's departments were compartmentalized. Intelligence professionals within its ranks didn't even know about the other directorates.

Yet here was Luke: fresh out of graduate school with no military experience. It wasn't a prerequisite for employment with the Company, but it helped. Although most who had military experience didn't have a master's degree. And now he found himself on the front lines of the Cold War.

As they headed toward the parking garage, John said, "We have a lot to discuss, Luke. First, I'm here to train you on the latest and greatest techniques we use. The stuff from your initial training is a bit outdated. Much of it is a throwback to the early days of American counterespionage—what the British taught us. We have new sales tactics and better incentives than the tired examples they use in a closed environment. Second, as you know, there is no guarantee that you have a future in this organization until you can prove to us that you have what it takes to operate on your own, possibly behind enemy lines, in their backyard."

John was a twenty-year veteran of the Cold War spy games. He started his career as an army counterintelligence special agent in the early days of Vietnam. He was the natural choice by the special agent in charge to take a new agent under his wing to ensure survival and success, just like Luke's professors and instructors. There was too much to lose from a tenderfoot agent running around Europe *sua sponte*.

John usually saw the same characters and personalities come through the Schoolhouse, the training facility outside Boston where all counterespionage agents were sent to learn their trade. Most were idealistic, eager to jump the gun on operations, and filled with ideas of grandeur. Luke was affable. He listened attentively to John and didn't interrupt while getting initial instructions. He was certainly not the popular quarterback with a heart of gold in high school who was central to every party or dance. He was the kid in the middle of the pack trying to figure out where he wanted his life to go after graduation. He was not the type to naturally lead others; he lacked the charisma needed to be a good politician or military leader, but because of his likeability, humility, and work ethic, others followed. He certainly wasn't born with the ability to grab people's attention or stand out from the pack, which made sense with his mediocre upbringing. His parents tried to be non-political, although they certainly leaned toward the left of the spectrum. They worked modest jobs and provided everything they could for their only child, but they were still lower middle-class. Luke had the usual opportunities of most American boys: Boy Scouts, football in the fall (second-string wide receiver), track in the spring, and even the stereotypical paper route when he was an adolescent. He obtained high marks throughout school and even through college, having graduated magna cum laude in international relations. He worked hard for those high marks but also found time for fun.

There seemed to be a renaissance for Luke in college through the magic of alcohol and lack of parents watching his every movement. When he went to fraternity parties a little inebriated, he came out of his shell. But when he sobered back up, he returned to where it was familiar: the middle of the pack. Because of those alcohol-fueled outbursts of charisma, his fraternity hailed him as most popular, and the sororities on campus agreed. It was his work ethic and positive attitude coupled with this newfound confidence during college that allowed him to impress his instructors at the Schoolhouse.

The Schoolhouse, however, recognized the shyness and slight uncertainty he had under the surface and worked with him to make the uncomfortable, sober, social situations a natural flow to which he could extract information from a target. Luke took to the Schoolhouse's icebreaker training module of FORD—Family, Occupation, Recreation, and Dreams—so he

A Mediocre Individual | 9

could keep up the small talk with strangers and build rapport with them. By the end of his nine months at the camp, he was able to walk across a room and make his target trust him. But that was in training with other Americans. Now he began on the long road to an odd career that did not come naturally but through intuition and experience, which his few years on earth lacked in all aspects, and he knew it.

"Things should go smoothly for your first coupla months. We've got defectors coming in faster than we can handle 'em." John briefed Luke as they speed away from the airport in a government-owned Citroen. Unlike the other government purchased vehicles, this Citroen was an off-orange instead of white. It also had local plates instead of diplomat plates normally used to keep the local security forces from stopping American personnel.

"We've got a defector from the other side of the Wall. His sister and her husband are dealin' with this KGB agent. The sister tells the agent she's got a brother, a real stand-up guy, who shares the same political views. Ya know, another Commie. So the agent figures why not recruit this guy too. Problem for the KGB is that this guy was trying to come over the Wall. For all his 'Ja, Commissar," he recognizes the folly of Communism. He wants to leave and start life anew in the United States."

Luke was wondering if he was up to the task laid before him. He had sudden doubts about his own abilities. What if he didn't learn as fast as he should; what would happen if he got a source killed? He tried to push those thoughts aside and focus on what John was briefing him on. John talked fast and used a lot of colloquialisms, but Luke did everything in his power to keep up with the briefing. He didn't want John to think he was a dullard after the praises he had received.

"So the guy says yes to the KGB and learns their tactics. He figured it would give him a bartering chip when he finally made it over. Problem for this dude is that we already have the information he's tryin' to sell. We turn him back to get more. This is gonna be your first mission. I'll introduce you two and see if you can't get him to play ball. I'll give you the reports tomorrow when we get to the office."

John pulled up to a new building. Even though the democratic West abhorred Communism, they used their building style to provide cheap housing after the bombing raids razed half of Berlin during World War II. The building was squared with six rows by six columns of windows—perfectly symmetrical and plain.

"We're two blocks north of here on the right side of the road. I'll be out front of the office in the morning to escort you inside. It will be difficult to get in when no one knows you but me," John instructed as he handed over a white letter-sized envelope. "Your lodging instructions and keys are all in there. Try to get a good night's sleep, Luke."

Luke began to plan for the worst-case scenario. Running through his mind, Luke had a burning decision to make: Should he see as many sights before he got fired, or should he put all his effort into the job? If he worked hard, he might leave on good terms, but then he would have missed out on the unique opportunity to see Europe before the Berlin Wall came down. How many mistakes could he make before they dismissed him? Luke tried to put those thoughts away again as he realized John was looking at him to make sure he was picking up what was being discussed. Luke shot John a half-cocked smile and a tilt of the head as he headed inside the apartment complex, almost disappointed in himself already.

The next morning started early for a jet-lagged Luke. He walked to the office and saw John already outside waiting by a running car.

"Hop in, Luke; we're heading out." Luke jogged to the car and hopped in. He was a bit jittery as he closed the car door. He thought it was his morning coffee sitting in his empty stomach, but that was just a lie he told himself. He knew John would be able to see fear or uncertainty in his actions. Luke also knew John and the rest of his coworkers were new once. He tried thinking this like a mantra. Instead of calming down, he just became more nervous. He began to focus on his shaking hand in his lap. He drew it in closer as he tried to look at John through his peripherals to see if he had noticed. Even though the morning air was cool, Luke could feel himself break a little sweat in his armpits and on his forehead. He didn't want to wipe away any sweat beads, but he didn't want them lingering there like a billboard for how nervous he was.

The Citroen's heater was on, but the engine was barely warm enough to heat the interior. A little bit of steam escaped John's lips as he let out a cough. Luke, on the other hand, looked like he had a boiling cup of water being held in his mouth as a cloud of smoke escaped with every breath.

After they drove for ten minutes, John pulled to the side of the road. "I'll be right back. Stay here."

John got out and walked to the adjacent bakery they had parked in front of. Luke was so nervous he didn't even notice where they had been or what was around him. John returned shortly with a small bag and two coffees. "Here, have something to eat; it'll help calm you down," John instructed.

Luke smiled that awkward, half-cocked smirk again. "Was it that obvious?" Luke shakily asked.

"You'll be fine, kid. Just breathe and think of your training."

"Excuse me, sir. But where are we heading?" Luke inquired.

"I got a call from the guy I told you about last night. He said he needs to meet."

"But... shouldn't I read the reports about this guy first? I mean, is there anything more I need to know about him?" Luke insisted. Now the sweat in his armpits and on his forehead began to form beads big enough to be subject to the laws of gravity. He could feel a bead rolling down his forehead as parts of his undershirt seemed to stick to him like drying glue.

"No time. He wants to meet this morning," John said as he drove, not even taking the time to look Luke in the eyes as he explained.

After another ten minutes of driving, John would stop the car and run inside a small store. Sometimes he told Luke to stay put and other times Luke was almost pulled from the car. This dance went on for two hours. They finally pulled into an alleyway on the wrong side of town and entered a small garage, where they both got out.

"This is it, Luke. We're meeting the source I told you about. I hope you remember what I told you about him," John said like a drill sergeant instructing a new private on hand grenade use. He was forceful but not belittling. "Because you're taking lead," John let out as he turned and led them into a small stairwell adjoining the garage.

Luke centered himself by recalling his training. "The source would not know everything I know. Why would he?" Luke thought to himself. "Unless John trained him well, which, with his years of experience, he probably did. How long has John been working with him? How intelligent is he? And John! John will be there, won't he?"

What Luke didn't know about John's experience was that it spanned twenty-plus years. He had been to Vietnam, Iran, Germany, and worked as part of the U.S. Army's COINTELPRO, or Counterintelligence Program, infiltrating Marxist and radical, left-leaning organizations in the United States. While operating in the COINTELPRO, John was at odds with his oath to the United States being used to weaponize agents into spying on other Americans. While his record was stellar, John felt, in hindsight, this was a black mark on his professional life. It seemed others did not feel that way, though. When people found out, they simply assumed he, and countless others, were doing a tough job on behalf of the American people.

While Luke was thinking about the task ahead of him, he was overcome by the possibilities awaiting him on the other side of the door. The thoughts flowed together so quickly Luke lost track of where he was for a moment. As the door to the meeting site opened, Luke kicked into high gear; no thoughts raced through his mind at all.

The introduction kicked off with the source looking nervous. His English was quite good, and after a short how-do-you-do handover, Luke put his training into action without even thinking about the next steps. He questioned the source and found a way to subtly request more information about this KGB agent. The source seemed a bit hesitant but agreed.

Luke gave the required training to the source, as well as requirements to fulfill when he returned to East Germany. The source seemed to appear able, although not the brightest of individuals, for the task at hand. Luke simplified things for the source so he was able to grasp the concept of how to obtain and record information as well as smuggle it across the border when he returned for their next meeting. After a long day, John and Luke separated from the source to allow him to go back to his natural habitat and carry out the tasks Luke had briefed him on.

"Holy shit, that took forever" said John. "Let's get a drink. You can meet the rest of the team."

Chapter 2

Practical Applications

Luke thought three o'clock in the afternoon was a bit early for a drink, but he didn't mind so much. John led Luke to a local bar, the office watering hole. The building looked as if it had survived bombing raids during World War II but had been standing there long before the 1940s. The mahogany bar and railings had been made with careful consideration and could probably stop a bullet. The bar was the centerpiece of the establishment, spanning the entire left side of the room. It stood in stark contrast to the cheap, modern, mass-produced tables and chairs that littered the front of the bar. As they walked toward the back of the establishment, Luke couldn't help but notice the Gothic archway that separated the front and back of the establishment. It was a shame someone had drilled into the century-old wood to hang ugly 1960s curtains up, which were no doubt used when patrons wanted a private affair.

"Grab us a couple of beers and head to the back; you'll see me and two others," John instructed. Luke got the beers and walked to the back, where he saw two other middle-aged guys smoking like chimneys. They looked tired and wired, like they'd been drinking coffee to keep going over the past twenty-four hours, while the bags under their eyes almost looked black and blue, as if they were in a fight. The dim lighting did not help their looks.

"Luke!" John yelled across the bar. "Guys, I want you to meet Luke, the prodigy we've heard so much about. Luke, this is Dave and Mike. They'll be looking over you to make sure you're getting along all right. They're good guys, experienced." The typical introductions were made and Luke took a seat as he drank his beer and listened to what the rest had to complain about with the daily endeavors of the job. About thirty minutes passed and the front door slammed. Everyone looked and gave an approving nod. The source walked to the table and gave a friendly hello.

"So I guess everyone else agrees on Luke's abilities?" asked the source in perfect English.

The table erupted in laughter. John broke in between giggles, "Yeah, everyone else finds him... adequate. He passed the test, wouldn't you say?"

Luke was baffled and had yet to realize the day's activities were a test to see how well he had learned at the Schoolhouse.

"Now the real fun begins," said John. "Luke, this is Willy."

Luke turned bright red with embarrassment but began to laugh uncontrollably. All this time he was so nervous he would screw up, and it turned out he was "adequate." He was in the middle of the pack again.

"It's William, dick," Willy said, shooting John a dirty look. "You're always breaking my balls, John." Willy was the site lead, an administrative head for the masters in Bamberg, Germany, and didn't get to play in the field anymore. So whenever new agents came in, he would sneak away from his desk and the incessant calls from headquarters and assess the new guys. Willy joined them, and they continued to swap stories, get to know Luke, and drink the night away.

"Let's get a shot, Luke," Willy said as he prompted Luke to go to the bar with him. "Why were you so nervous today? What was going through your mind when John said you were going to take lead?" Waiting for an answer, Willy took down his shot of what looked like vodka.

"Well, I just... didn't want to disappoint anyone, or myself, I guess," Luke stammered out as he started to take his shot. The odd choice of gin burned Luke's throat as it made its way down, and his face showed it.

"The whole time, Luke, it looked like you had a secret to tell, like you were hiding something and wanted to yell it from the rooftops. Don't let your secret show, Luke. Just use that feedback to get better at your trade," Willy advised as he grabbed his beer and headed back toward the guys. Over the next half hour everyone ran out of steam, and money. So they all stumbled back to the apartments, ready to reset for the next day.

The next morning Luke and John met for breakfast at a café one block away from the apartment to begin assessment and training. John was unusually sober for having drunk so much the night before. Luke was still a little drunk but did everything he could to appear sober. He knew he was going to bed as soon as he was done for the day, and that was enough to keep him going. John knew what Luke felt but also knew it was necessary for Luke to learn how to be a responsible agent, as well as stand up for himself; he could have left at any time or refused the next drink.

Luke had the familiar signs of a new agent after a night of drinking: sunglasses on, sitting away from the sun, bags under his eyes big enough not to be covered by the sunglasses. And of course, he was still jet-lagged from the trip over two days before. Luke didn't even take the time to shave for the day.

"So what're they teachin' at the Schoolhouse nowadays?" John asked as part of the assessment. Being a counterespionage agent wasn't just gathering information or eliminating threats but also required the ability to articulate any given situation as succinctly as possible.

"They taught us the usual tricks of picking locks, parachuting, communications and, of course, writing the appropriate reports for what was discovered through talking to people with knowledge."

"There we go. Let's explore that skill. Ya see that girl over there reading the book? I want you to get her name and phone number." John nodded toward the front bar, where a blonde sat reading a small book. She wore a white-and-blue sundress while she enjoyed a warm drink with an orange slice on the rim and a cinnamon stick adorning the steam circling about the air.

Practical Applications | 25

"You want me to pick her up? She doesn't look like she wants to be hit on at nine in the morning."

"You're not gonna marry her! Get the info. If she doesn't want to talk, then it makes the task that much more difficult. What's your approach?"

"Well, I have a map of the city, a pen, a camera, and 150 Deutsche Marks."

"Leave the money out of it. Use it if you need to buy a Coke or something, but don't bribe her."

"OK, I'll ask for directions."

"What are you doing in West Berlin?"

"I work for Coca-Cola."

"What about the camera?"

"I'm sightseeing. I don't have a meeting until tomorrow."

"Who's the guy you're with?"

"A coworker. This is my first trip with the company, and he isn't too interested in sightseeing because he's been to Germany before..."

"If he's been to Germany before, then why does she need to give you directions?" John smugly sipped from his glass as he awaited a response with some good logic to it.

"He only goes to the bars and business meetings. He has no interest in such cultural items."

"Let's see if it works," John stated as if to give permission for Luke to pick up a strange girl.

Luke got up and approached the girl. Shaky with his German, and nervous as to his true intentions, he started looking flustered. He tried to remember the advice Willy had given him the night prior.

"Guten Morgen, Fräulein. Sprechen Sie Englisch?"

"Ja, I speak some," she fired back, having barely looked at Luke.

Luke asked directions to the Charlottenburg Palace. This allowed her to interact enough for Luke to figure her out. Was she upset, willing to help, just being polite, or would she blow him off completely? The girl was polite and helped him but made little eye contact and didn't offer much more than what Luke had asked for. Luke asked the history of the tall obelisk readily seen through the café's front window, an obvious ploy to keep her talking.

"It is the Berlin Victory Column," she huffed at him. "Is this the reason you ask for directions? To get tour of city?" the young woman asked angrily as she rolled her head toward Luke and made solid eye contact for the first time in their interaction.

"Although I need the directions, I do have ulterior reasons to speak to you."

"And what are those reasons?" she asked with a smirk.

"I'm in town for a short while and would like to understand your country and its history."

"Isn't Hitler enough for you Americans to know?"

Luke was lost. Had he offended her, or was she testing him? Was there a way to rebound from this setback?

"I understand Germany fought off the Romans. This is the history I'm interested in, if you can stand talking to an American."

"Most Americans I meet do not know this about Germany."

"Well, I'm not most Americans," Luke said as he slowly made himself comfortable at her table, taking the chair opposite her as he continued the conversation. He looked over her shoulder and saw a sandwich delivered to John as he looked content to read his newspaper. Luke used this as a cue to continue his line of questioning.

Luke thought through his Rolodex of training to search feverishly for a way to keep the conversation going. "FORD: Family!" Luke had the tools to complete the job; he just needed to put them into action correctly. If he was too blunt, it may scare her away; too subtle and the technique may not work. "I wish my parents could see these sights like I am. I feel pictures don't do this city justice. Do you find your family enjoys the splendors this city has to offer, or does it just feel like home to you?"

Luke gave himself a high-five in his head. The conversation was going just as he wanted it to. Through the whole encounter, he centered himself by repeating, "It's just directions, it's just directions. This is natural for people."

Luke used family and recreation, as he felt discussing her occupation and dreams was too much for a first interaction. They spoke until Luke saw John tapping his watch and paying the bill. Luke offered to pay for the girl's orange cinnamon apple cider and asked for her phone number. She thanked Luke for the drink as she slid a piece of paper to his side of the table.

"Until next time," she said in a low voice, with a gentle smile escaping her lips.

As Luke walked back to John's table, a smile broke out on his face.

"Mission accomplished."

"Good job. You seemed a lot more natural than yesterday. Willy must've given you one hell of a pep talk to make that reversal happen," John supposed. "Now you need to establish recontact."

"So... you want me to date her, basically."

"Well, you don't have to go steady, if that's what you're worried about. The point is to use your environment to hone your craft. That's the point of this; she thinks you're dating, you're running through the source steps. And don't forget, Luke, never fall in love with your source." John put his sunglasses on and looked back at Luke. "Don't forget the reports, either; we want details. C'mon, the day is still early. I'll drive today; we'll take your driving lessons slow."

John took Luke on a city tour: cafés, shops, alleyways, good takeout, bad takeout, West Berlin checkpoints, hospitals, all the things someone knew about their environment when they lived there. In between attractions, John asked about training, doctrine, and personalities who may have taught Luke at the Schoolhouse, and he used the time with him to delve into Luke's personality through small talk, which further built rapport. After about nine hours about town, John pulled up to Luke's apartment.

"It's been a long day for you. Get a good night's sleep. We'll meet again at the office in the morning—8:30, but be a little early."

Luke's training had prepared him for the life he was about to step into, as much as one could be prepared for the lifestyle. His upbringing sure did him no favors for the rigors of the real world and responsible adulthood. He was surrounded by burned-out counterculture activists who were crushed by reality when their free love resulted in the responsibility of children. Although his parents and their friends were not overt in their political beliefs, they would certainly allude to their left-leaning tendencies and criticisms of conservative American politics. They did let comments about the military-industrial complex slip from time to time. He watched as the world changed around him in the aftermath of the Vietnam War and again toward American prosperity in the era of greed—from long hair and drug use in the late 1960s to ponytails and discussions of stock swaps toward the end of his academic career in the early '80s.

Luke was mediocre as a Boy Scout but did make Eagle Scout. He was middle of the pack on the track team and good enough at football to be second string but never good enough to be first. He wasn't very impressive on first glance: nice enough to get along with but not too memorable. He was called average and unremarkable by his coaches and teachers but lauded for this quality during his counterespionage training. He had that gray man factor necessary to gain trust, obtain information needed, and leave with no one asking about his presence. He never spoke about his political beliefs or took an outward stance on provocative topics. People enjoyed him being around, but he wasn't called if a group was going out. In college, a state school, he had to study to attain those high marks that earned him his cum laude honors. At the same time, he didn't have to burn the midnight oil or cram for exams to ensure a barely passing grade. He had quite a few dates with various sisters from the lesser-known sorority houses. Most were nice girls who enjoyed Luke taking them to a museum for a first date instead of the usual dinner and a movie followed with a quick pass to wrap up the evening with sex.

In fact, he never slept with a girl on the first date. Luke was, by all accounts, mediocre and forgettable.

Luke was part of the next generation of patriots and starkly different from John, who was born into the nuclear family concept while the world was at war against Imperial Japan and Nazi Germany. His mother had worked in an airplane factory while his father island-hopped in the Pacific with the army. When his father returned home, he had a tough time adjusting back to civilian life and took it out on John's brothers and mother. John fit the mold of the stereotypical middle child and did everything he could to make peace in the house. A natural leader who took charge when no one else would, and sometimes when they did, he was able to think quickly on his feet and make decisions for a positive outcome. It often seemed John had the next move ready even when the previous one had not presented itself yet. John grew up in an America still celebrating its victory from World War II. The stories from his uncles about life overseas filled John with patriotism and wanderlust, which was why he enlisted in the army. But he didn't want to be just any soldier; hearing of the exploits of the Office of Strategic Services, he wanted to take on dangerous missions, which led him to volunteer in the counterintelligence corps. John had no interest in college but realized it meant he would never be an officer. He was fine with being enlisted because he knew his chances of fieldwork were almost assured, as the officers were needed in the rear echelons conducting administrative tasks. But then he heard of a new type of outfit lauded by President Kennedy, the Special Forces, and he knew they would need intelligence support. He sought out an assignment by selling his capabilities to the commander of a unit bound for a nation in Southeast Asia little-known to many Americans at that time: Vietnam. After serving six years in the army, three of them as an adviser in Vietnam, he got out and sought to take the fight to the Communists out of uniform. John's wanderlust took him from the jungles of Southeast Asia to the 1968 Democratic National Convention, Iran, and the concrete jungles of central Europe.

"I'll see you at the office tomorrow at 8:30, Luke," John said as he dropped Luke off at his apartment. The building had many tenants; among them were Mike and Dave. Being habitual late-night drinkers, they knocked on Luke's door.

"We're having our nightly ritual. Why don't you join us?" Mike asked when Luke opened the door. Although Mike wasn't invited in yet, the spirits of Jack Daniel's felt comfortable enough to swirl about the air of the entrance way and creep their way past Luke as if on their way to the kitchen looking for ice to make the next drink. Not wanting to be rude or seem like a lightweight, he invited them in to drink. Luke didn't have any drinks or groceries in the apartment yet, but Dave had conveniently brought half a bar worth of alcohol and mixers.

"So what should I expect tomorrow at work?" Luke asked as the guys melted into the cheap government seats that furnished the living room.

He took the opportunity to get to know them through eliciting the office politics.

They both looked like they had some life experience. Or they just didn't take very good care of themselves. They were both carrying a little extra weight. Dave looked like he might have been a high school or college track star, but years of drinking and a high-stress job had left him with a little pot belly and a bad combover concealing his thinning black hair, which was held in place by copious amounts of hair grease. This wasn't flattering to his thin frame and 5'7" stature. Mike was a bit more robust, like he may have played football in his younger years. His drinking didn't take as bad a toll on his gut, but the habitual smoking caused him to sporadically catch his breath when he got flustered or got too in-depth with a war story. He was blessed with better genes in the hair department, though. His thick brown hair was kept short on the sides and only long enough on top to let others know his hair was curly. His horn-rimmed glasses were a throwback to the 1960s but comprised a style he was accustomed to; he refused to give in to the latest optical fashion trends.

"Truth is, you'll be the reports bitch for a little bit. At least until you show your knowledge on the adversary. When you do get the chance to go into the field, it'll be shadowing someone. Unless an investigation comes up," Mike explained between hiccups as he mixed himself another drink in the kitchen.

"Drink up, kid," he said as he handed Luke a Jack and Coke, which Luke found contained more Jack than Coke.

"How often do investigations happen here?" Luke inquired. He was eager to get down to the nitty-gritty of the job, be it informant operations or investigations.

"Rarely, at most," bellowed Dave from the seat it seemed he was now one with.

Luke listened attentively as Dave and Mike talked about life, the office, the job, and the issues they felt plagued world politics. Mike and Dave had homesteaded in Germany by turning down promotions and didn't want to go back to the United States. They cited protestors and antigovernment sentiment as their reasoning, but Luke knew those days were over. No longer were service members spat on when they returned home; protests and dead students at Kent State were a thing of the past. Luke sensed they were just having too much fun running about Europe spying and drinking. Plus there was extra money to be made overseas—not much, just enough to make it worthwhile to stay there over taking promotions and commensurate raises.

It was a whirlwind day for Luke. Dave and Mike promised more days like it. They encouraged him to call the girl from the coffee shop and see the sights, and according to Mike, Luke had to see Rome. It was a short flight away, after all. Luke went to bed with optimistic thoughts for the future and what he hoped would be a long career. The nagging feeling of inadequacies melted away as the confidence he had acquired during college violently sprang forth.

Chapter 3

Basic Training

Luke walked from his apartment to the nondescript two-story office building where he had met John the previous day. It was a beige, almost cream color with evenly spaced windows and a brown double door centered on the side of the building facing the street. It was new around the time of World War I but had been refurbished once before and once since World War II. The windows opened downward instead of split in half, and it had always served as an office complex since its inception. The first floor used to house a factory of some sort based on the vaulted ceilings and archways emplaced on the alley side of the structure; they were the original loading docks for horse-drawn carriages making deliveries when the building started its life. A large brass placard was affixed to the upper left of the entrance with business names on it: Schmidt Veröffentlichung, a small publishing firm; Frank Investitionen, an investment house; Hugo Boss clothier; Uniform Services; DHL shipping; and Nähere Telekommunikation, or Closer Telecommunications—NT, as the team would call it. They worked in this second-story business, from which their communications support staff made house calls and fixed telephones. The business also "discovered new and exciting technologies relating to mobile communications." This was a clever ruse to hide their true intent of fighting the Soviets.

NT looked like a typical communications support firm. Upon entering there were desks with computers, typewriters, and stacks of papers—invoices mostly. Some desks were cluttered with telephone parts, tools, or manuals in

English and German. The desks were aligned on either wall with equal spacing, making a path down the center of them. At the end of the room was the manager's office. To the right of that door was another labeled *Maintenance*. John escorted Luke into the maintenance room.

"This is where the magic happens," said John.

Inside the rather large maintenance room was another door, which opened to the real reason behind this foreign business venture. This was the headquarters of their local operations. John escorted Luke down a narrow corridor with three small rooms off the left side. The first room they passed had radios set up from floor to ceiling. There were two men inside casually dressed, smoking, and drinking coffee as if their lives depended on it. The sound of men speaking Russian could be heard between the annoying static that accompanies radio communications.

As John and Luke continued down the corridor, the second door revealed a small room the guys referred to as "the crash shack." Two olive-drab army cots were set up against the wall with a blanket and pillow on each. There was a countertop with a coffee station and the usual accompaniments of powdered cream, sugar packets, and plastic stirrers. Next to this was a large safe with five drawers and a dial lock from which two handmade signs hung. One declared, "Dry Goods Only," the second, "Do *Not* Lock." As it turned out, this five-hundred-pound safe, designed and purchased to hold classified information, was put hard to work holding snacks. Next to the safe was a medium-size off-white refrigerator with another handmade sign exclaiming, "If You Didn't Put It In, Don't Take It Out!" Posted around the sign on the refrigerator were Polaroids of women.

John half turned to Luke as they walked. "If you can follow through, your girl will get up on the wall of fame too."

"Heartbreakers and life takers, huh?"

"Heartbreakin' is only a hobby, and life takin's for the army, kid. We just get information and send reports," John retorted as he escorted

Luke to the rest of the office. "Here we are: the bullpen."

John and Luke walked into the last office. It was not unlike the front office: desks, telephones, typewriters, and papers strewed about. They even had two computers for file keeping. This office, however, had maps on the walls and a chalkboard with lines connecting names, pictures, and places, along with notes on the side with theories on how everything meshed together. Mike and Dave were already sitting in the office, half working and half debating politics. Even with their late-night ritual, they still managed to perform in top shape, despite what tales their physiques may tell. They compared world leaders to women with interwoven profanities that made the conversation so convoluted that it was hard to determine whether they were still talking about politics or women from their past.

"Gentlemen, you remember the Fucking New Guy. FNG, you remember Mike and Dave."

Luke shook hands with the men and gave a sheepish nod of acknowledgment mixed with amazement at how they were there early and sober.

"You and I will have to work from the same desk for now. We requisitioned more furniture, but who the hell knows when that'll get in." John pointed to a desk in the corner. It was littered with paperwork and what must have been three packs worth of cigarettes in an overfilled ashtray.

"Hey, FNG, coffee's getting low!" bellowed Mike, as a smirk escaped his attempt at stoicism. Luke could tell from the previous night's discussion that Mike had enough salt to teach him the finer points of the job but not as much as John. Mike looked as if he had shaved that morning but already had a five o'clock shadow. He wore cheap suits as well as too much cologne in an attempt to cut through and cover up the cigarette smoke.

"Anybody need a cup?" asked Luke. He knew his place in the firm and wanted to let everyone else know it didn't bother him. No one answered Luke's inquiry, so he walked out to the adjacent break room to attend to his new duties.

"What do you think so far, John? Think this probie has what it takes?" asked Dave in a hushed tone as soon as Luke left the room. He was the last addition to the team, having joined two years before, and was critical of everyone who passed through the office. This cynicism, in addition to his time in the marines, gave him a gritty edge that repelled most people. At least when he was sober.

"He seems... affable." John always hesitated to make conclusions, because that's what twenty years in the job had shown was best policy.

Mike spoke up. "He's young. Real young, John. I know we all bad-mouth the college students with no experience, but I think he may have a future here, pending the rest of his probationary status, of course." Mike always passed judgment and then amended it with a disclaimer for future failures.

Luke walked back into the office with a cup of coffee, fully aware the guys had just been talking about him. He did not want to come off as nervous, but he could not stand the silence in the office, either. He searched his repertoire to come up with an icebreaker topic. His training told him to look around and use the environment to blend in. While camouflage was important for soldiers, intelligence agents needed to look like they belonged to their surroundings. Looking around the room, he noticed a lack of calendars, pictures, or hobby items someone may have left out. Not one periodical was present for his use. Just then, another common interest came to mind.

"Coffee's done, if anybody wants a cup. I usually make it strong. So tell me what you think. You know, so I can adjust it. Or..." Luke sheepishly trailed off, waiting for someone else to pick up the conversation.

"Thanks, Luke," said John casually. "Why don't we get down to business, though? I want to brief you on what's been happening so you can tag along and meet some of our sources. Not immediately, but just in case." Luke and John took a seat at the desk where a large file lay. "This is a roll-up of our latest and greatest. Did they tell you about this list at the Schoolhouse?"

"They didn't tell us much there, except to ask questions and call the lawyers if we're unsure about an action." Luke regurgitated the phrase to come up with something witty.

"I see we went to the same course!" Mike said jokingly as he stood over the desk. "They didn't tell us shit we could use either. Between John, Dave, and me, you'll get the skills necessary to succeed. We're here for you, troop!"

Everyone rolled their eyes and let out a chuckle. These colloquialisms were used to advertise their time in the military. It was not a conscious effort but rather conditioning acquired through a system that stripped a person of their individualism and replaced it with buzzwords such as *esprit de corps*, *duty*, and *honor*. These were the things a new agent with no military experience lacked and needed to be reconditioned from their cushy life as a private citizen to one as a public servant.

Part of conditioning Luke, or any new counterespionage agent, was to endow them with a realistic understanding of when they had been beaten. A good counterespionage agent needed to understand when the battle was lost and to regroup for a new offensive without pride or prejudice against the adversary. But another part of this reconditioning was understanding there were no Hollywood endings; there were no grand parades when a good job was done, or when the individual struck a major victory. Everyone in the office would take the credit, because everyone would have helped in some way. What Luke also failed to realize was the job made the players work in the shadows, look over their shoulders in a silent fear they were being hunted, and retain enough discipline to deny everything if they were caught.

"OK, so here's what we've got: This dossier catalogues seven sources; four are working for us and three are being developed. The group of four is working inside the KGB as support personnel mostly, and are hoping to work with us in exchange for safe passage to the U.S. We have a building maintenance supervisor, a cryptographer, a secretary to the Berlin station chief, and a Russian intelligence soldier; he monitors traffic on shortwave radios, mostly. The three being developed are lower in the chain and a good start for you. Ah, this one, the janitor..."

"A janitor? I don't expect to handle a big fish, but what's a janitor going to do for us?" Luke blurted out.

"You tell me. What *can* a janitor do for us?" John tested Luke with the ability to take the hard sell and run with it. "Where does he work?"

Luke flipped open the dossier and thumbed through a couple pages. "East Berlin Foreign Minister's Office."

Leaning back in his chair while taking another sip of coffee, John asked, "How deep into the building can he access?"

"Ahhhh... hold on... unknown," Luke said as he continued to flop the dossier around in his hands. The folder opened like a book, but each page had to be flipped over the top, making it hard for him to switch between report sections.

"Do the Soviets trust him to be around secret information?"

"Unknown."

"Is he pro-U.S.?"

"The report writer says he is. I need to find out what he can do for us. Does he have an education, what's his maturity level, does he have a family that motivates him? How well is he known around the building? Maybe he's good with mechanical items, like, say, locks and cameras."

"It sounds like you have a plan, Luke. Start putting it on paper. Mike will make the introduction when you and the janitor are primed. In the meantime, when's your date?"

"What date? With the girl at the statue this morning?"

"I told you we want details. Get basic information on who she is and find a way to confirm it. In the meantime, what do you know about the current political situation between us and the Soviets?"

This topic of conversation brought everyone in for discussion. John started off with what had happened between the U.S. and Soviets by way of Vietnam. Now it was up to the U.S. to return the favor in Afghanistan. Guerrilla warfare between the Russians and the Mujahedeen were funded by the CIA and carried out with Pakistani backing. Stinger missiles had not yet turned the tide of the war but were on their way. Moscow was more focused on the shooting war, leaving gaps in the European theater. The Soviets had discovered a U.S. listening posts in a tunnel under Berlin and used this in the fight of counterintelligence. When the Soviets had their fill, they killed U.S. agents behind the Iron Curtain and exposed the tunnel to the world in an attempt to paint the U.S. in a bad light politically. In reality, no one cared. It was business as usual.

"So what's in place now that the tunnels were compromised?" asked Luke.

"Human intelligence," Dave chimedin. "Aggressive recruitment of sources. That's why it's so important for you to understand the best way of finessing the proper people to agree with capitalism over Communism. If done wrong, you're compromised or killed; if done right, we get information to stop the Soviets."

"There are tunnels still not discovered, but they have to be mothballed for the time being. Our guys have filled them with ballast to throw off any sonar traces of cavitations in the earth. When we can confirm it's safe again, they'll resume operations," John informed Luke.

Dave and Mike went back to sundry tasks that awaited them on their desks. John began to shuffle paperwork.

"OK, Luke," John started. "From now on the tests and exercises we're gonna give you are overt; no more trickery on our part." John needed to make sure Luke was trained properly. Chess can be a challenge, but at least there's only one opponent and rules to govern the game. In Cold War Berlin, the rules were fast and loose. John did not have space on the team for someone who was not prepared to do battle in the world of espionage and counterespionage.

John assigned Luke a research project involving analytics of the adversary. "I want you to draft a threat brief about the Stasi, the East German secret police force. They *are* the front lines of overt action in East Berlin. Include all their capabilities, weapons, overview of tactics, and leadership. When the report is finished, you'll brief the rest of the office, take questions, and receive a critique. After we call the end to the exercise, we'll go around the horn and give you some feedback and additional information you may not have picked up in your research." John walked Luke down the hall and showed him the records cabinet for all the previous reports filed against a country or organization.

"Now, I believe you have a phone call to make to a certain young lady," John reminded Luke.

"But don't I have a report due, sir?" Luke asked, looking confused.

"You went to college, Luke," John said accusingly. "Multitask. You will have to juggle different cases, reports, administrative tasks, and sources. This should be a good warm-up."

Luke sat at the closest desk, called the number on the napkin, and set a date.

The next morning everyone arrived at the office and found Luke finishing a document. "If there's time today, John, I think I have all I need on the Stasi," Luke stated without a hello. He beamed with pride at his hard work. Poor Luke got torn to shreds on the presentation. It was not so much the information contained in the report; it was the *lack* of information in the report. Luke had a long way to go before becoming a subject-matter expert.

Once the guys disappeared back into the cloud of cigarette smoke or to the break room for a fresh cup of coffee or to go back to their desks to pretend they were hard at work, Luke approached John. "Also, here's the report from my date, John, as requested."

"Not a date, a meeting; it was a meeting. Give me a few chapters, not the whole book," John growled as he blew on his fourth cup of coffee for the day.

"She's twenty-four, not enthusiastic about U.S. policy but willing to listen to an American; she's intellectual, went to university, and graduated with a bachelor's degree..."

"What's the degree in?" John interrupted.

"Renaissance art," Luke shot out. He hesitated before going on without a prompt from John. "She has a studio apartment and a cat."

"Studio apartment, eh?" John smirked as he looked up from his coffee. "How did you confirm?"

"The details are in the report. And the photos on the fridge, sir."

John looked up with an impressed look on his face. "You move fast, kid. Just don't get too attached. And think about the overall collection mission."

"I just got to know her. Nothing happened between us other than talking, sir," Luke stated, correcting John in his assumption they had slept together. "Besides, I want to hang on to her for more information about the sights of the city. What I don't want is to find out she's part of a group that may compromise my clearance."

Looking back at Luke, John nodded his head in approval. "Well, it looks like you're on the right path, kid." John changed the subject to the day's work and instructed Luke to start looking over the backlog of field reports. This was John's job as the senior agent, but the tedious work of correcting minor grammatical errors and formatting according to headquarters' weekly changes usually meant he sometimes overlooked the real meat and potatoes of the report. "If you need anything, just holler," he advised as he took a sip of his coffee and walked away.

John walked into the break room to look at the picture Luke had obtained. If he didn't sleep with her, then the picture should be benign. Hanging squarely on the freezer door, away from the other photos, was a Polaroid of a young lady and Luke sitting outside a café at dusk.

Chapter 4

Secretarial Duty

Over the next three weeks, Luke plugged away at the ever-growing stack of reports that came in from the field. Some were about source meetings, detailing the personalities and habits of the individuals recruited, or potentially recruited, to give information to the United States government. Sources' hobbies, language capabilities, ability to collect information, and motivations to work with the United States instead of the Communist factions were all assessed. Some were about intelligence collected during those meetings: Soviet troop movements, agents they had in the field, threats to American forces and their European Allies. Some were about people who looked attractive enough to potentially be recruited for honeypot operations as well as a few suspected homosexuals for blackmail operations. They did not read like James Bond novels but rather dry, doctrinal, fact-based thrillers. They excited and bored the reader. But Luke liked the boredom they offered. He was aware these reports, when put together, would indicate the Soviets' next move in their efforts to overthrow capitalism. These briefs' aggregate information would form a one-paragraph report briefed to the vice president of the United States, after all! Luke made sure the reports were as accurate as possible, with corroborating reports from other agents.

Sometimes Luke had to assess if the writer was overlooking some negative trait about the source. He had to look for answers to such questions as, "Is there too personal a relationship between the field collector and source?" Or "Is the field collector desperate to keep the source, even when the source is not producing results?" Was the field collector being duped by the source? Did the collector know it? Were they not connecting the dots to see the big picture? These were all efforts vital to keeping the field collector, and the source, safe. Above all, the American life going out to obtain information was more important, but the source's life needed to be protected too. Luke found some comfort in knowing he may find some information that would directly affect field operations.

Luke enjoyed the work environment but felt his heart sink a little when he overheard the morning brief from Dave, Mike, or John about their day's meetings. They talked through what motivated their sources and the ensuing sales pitch they threw at them each time they met. These talks kept their sources motivated to spy; what route they would take to ensure they were not followed; and what they needed to compensate their source, should there be any funds or special services required. Some sources wanted to go to the United States with their families, so arrangements were made to justify the State Department's decision to allow for such immigration. Luke dreamed of his chance to get out there in the field, behind the Wall. And the reports aided in his ideas of grandeur. As he heard what the other agents were doing and read their ensuing reports, he imagined himself on the front lines, alone and unafraid.

The reality is that no agent was truly alone or unafraid. That's why they kept doing the job. It was dangerous and paid little. Deep inside them, unspoken but understood by their fellow agents, was a fear of being caught. Despite that fear, they reveled in the chance to be on the front lines of espionage. It provided a quiet adrenaline rush. If they were caught, the United States government would eventually fess up to them being one of theirs and attempt a spy swap, but it often took years to get them back. Meanwhile they waited out the legal proceedings through diplomatic channels in a Soviet gulag, subject to round-the-clock interrogations or, if the Soviets already had the information they wanted, torture.

An agent's release could take years. And while agents may have often gone into the field alone, they were backed by a team ready to come to their aid at short notice to prevent the loss of one of their own.

On a morning of no import, Luke came into the office eager to share some analytics he had discovered from the previous day's reports. The walk in to work seemed normal; transitioning from the front office to the secretive work area seemed normal; the smell of reheated morning coffee seemed normal. Luke went to his desk and snagged up his notes from the previous night. He hurriedly walked to the office next door to talk to the rest of the guys about his discovery.

"I think I found something of interest from yesterday's reporting that substantiates what another report said," Luke blurted out as he walked into the office without a hello. As he looked up, everyone was standing around like they had just found out their dog had died. Some had coffee cups in their hand, but they weren't drinking. Some had lit cigarettes but weren't smoking them, as the long lines of ash on the ends indicated.

"Uhh... yeah, yeah. Go ahead, Luke," John said as he looked down at the floor. Luke laid out what he felt was a momentous discovery. No one said a word. No one asked any questions. No one moved or reacted to Luke. Luke thought John and the guys would be pleased to hear what he had discovered, but there was a tension in the air. Luke knew something was headed his way, if not for the entire office. It was their smoldering cigarettes sitting between their fingers with half an inch of ash that first alerted Luke. They were smoking as usual. Coffee was made as usual. But the coffee was sitting cold in their cups and the cigarettes weren't being smoked. It seemed Luke was five minutes late to the breaking news.

"Good, good. I'll read it over. Look... something's come up. HQ is asking for someone to go across the Wall. Problem is that we've all been compromised; or at least that's what's being reported over the wire from one of our sources. We're compromised. All of us. Except you."

Mike took a long drag of his burning cigarette while the ash fell all over his suit. Luke could tell by the pause and long silence that what would follow next was not approved of through the office.

"I am in receipt of a directive that states I send *you* into East Germany. We need a fresh face to take the reins on this one, Luke." There was deep concern in John's voice, a bit shaky, a bit on the verge of cursing out his anger. "At this point you've been found to be favorable, even though you lack the proper training and experience. Do you think you can keep your cool on this, Luke?"

This was his "alone and unafraid" moment, but all he could feel was anxiety. He was being tasked with going into enemy territory. He had been trained, but just enough to get his ass kicked in a bar fight. After being around the guys and discussing the trade with them, Luke knew he was not trained enough for this. But still, he waited for the next step, some sort of instructions, but all he heard was the intense sound of his own pulse in his ears. He looked up, and John's face ripped Luke back to the calm present.

"I'm willing if I'm needed. But I must ask, sir, what is the task?"

"We need you to go across and extract a source that's been compromised. We think he has more information, but he needs to be debriefed as soon as possible. But it also involves debriefing another asset, a safe-house keeper. This is a simple snatch-and-run job. Should take about two days to get all the info, get the source, and get back here to safety. Are you up for it, Luke?"

"Anything at all, sir," Luke forced out as his throat dried up and he felt his body temperature spike.

"Good. Atta boy, Luke," John said with a lack of confidence. While he gave some reassuring words to Luke, John was looking down at the ground, as if he didn't want to look Luke in the eyes as he signed his death warrant. "Last night we got a call from the Mechanic on the emergency line. He works at the Russian embassy over there, and he said there was movement to take out American spies. Last week one of the Soviets' mothballed tunnels was opened and resumed operation. The Mechanic said there has been radio equipment coming into the embassy and he overheard a secretary talking about the need for jail cells and interrogators to come from Moscow. We know they have Stasi interrogators available, but for the in-depth stuff they send captives to Moscow; that's a good sign—preparation of local jail cells. But when they come here, it means there's going to be executions."

Right then a phone rang. Everyone but John and Luke left to go back to work. Willy entered with more news from HQ.

"It looks like you made a compelling argument, John," Willy said as he turned to Luke. "It looks like you got seventy-two hours reprieve, kid. John, I want you to get him ready. Or as ready as you can get him for this mission. Don't forget to let him sleep."

John and Luke started right away.

Chapter 5

The Mission

Luke received three days of classes that focused on the exact skills he would need to handle this mission. Since other, unpredictable issues would likely arise, he was also given a class on surreptitious communications. When he ran into a decision requiring higher-echelon policy makers, he would be able to communicate the issue and receive a directive back to execute. The communications support shop gave him a class on antenna theory and how to apply it to the improvised field radio class as well. A plan was established within the shop for what Luke should and should not say, how to say it, and when to say it when over the Wall. He signed for 5,000 Deutsche Marks, converted from the American coffers to be spent on the local economy.

He was given a cover story: He was a mechanical engineer, a skill close to his heart, as it was what his father had a degree in. Luke recalled growing up. His father always impressed upon his son the need for education and the collective efforts of academic thought. It was something his father was exposed to in college, and he applied the notion wherever he went. Luke was to say he was crossing to aid the Trabant factory in their efforts to sell cars to the West, which would interest the Soviets due to their wasteful spending and policies that stifled capitalism. For how much they hated capitalism, their military efforts required money that could only come from increased revenue. As the Cold War went on, the Soviets' policies were forced to conform to the idea of open trade—as long as the money garnered went to the proletariat, of course. Despite their ideas of equality, those at the top of the political chain lived lavish lifestyles while the common citizen lived in destitution. Another reason to promote foreign income. Luke's cover would allow that foreign income. The Trabant would no longer be an option only to the Soviet states. Luke studied the dossier of the source, the Mechanic, to know what he liked and disliked; to know the communications plan to authenticate whether he had the right source; to know what might offend him, so Luke would not say the wrong thing and destroy rapport or cause a ruckus to ensue that might alert local authorities.

Luke went through pre-mission planning with Mike. He pulled a map of East Berlin out for Luke to use. As usual, Luke was responsible for making his own route, and Mike, acting as guide and instructor, would critique it so it would be refined for Luke to study, remember, and use on the night of the mission. Luke had to make one route into the safe house and one back to NT from the safe house.

"Don't forget to stop and see Ingrid," Mike instructed. Ingrid was a source NT used frequently to get a handle on any last-minute information the office may not have had. She held the "go-ahead" information all agents used when they passed over for extended missions. If the Soviets were moving in any manner, she knew about it and passed the information along to NT agents so they could determine if they should continue with the operation.

Ingrid had been a source for NT since she was seventeen. She was tall and thin but not skinny. While she was considered attractive by conventional standards, she had worked as a source for ten years, so the agents treated her more like a sister than a source or potential lover. They all wished her the best in Soviet territory. While agents were confident their capitalist society would ultimately win over Soviet Communism, they also harbored some doubt and hoped Ingrid would be OK. But they also knew what historically happened to spies in the end.

"This doesn't make any sense, Luke. Where are you going on these streets? What are you stopping for? You do plan on stopping, right?" Mike critiqued Luke's final products.

"From the map, this seems good. I thought…" Luke looked at the map with red lines drawn all over to see with an analytical eye if he had in fact made a route with no logic to it. Biting his lip, tilting his head, and letting out a groan, he asked, "This looks good but doesn't support what I'm doing there late at night, assuming I'm leaving at night, right? Mike?"

Mike took another look and confirmed, "The directions look good, but I know this part of the city." He pointed to an area adjacent to the Berlin Wall. "This area looks like apartments but is really surveillance sites established to keep an eye on the West. And the East. They keep an eye on both sides of the wall due to their paranoia of defectors to the right side. Driving through there at night will look odd. Change that up. The rest will have to suffice, given the lack of shops and businesses open during the time you're supposed to go over."

Luke nodded and changed that portion of his route. Mike reminded Luke of his appointment with the Toy Shop, where he would get his field equipment issued to him. He was sent to the Fünfte Straße, or Fifth Street, front company to acquire his toys. This would be his James Bond–meets–Q moment. The Fifth Street front was a run-down auto shop that improvised vehicles and field equipment, such as firearms, radios, listening devices, and beacons used in tracking. There, Luke met Franz, a local German who was recruited to run the shop and gave training to agents on the latest and greatest gadgets his efforts produced. Luke met Franz in the research and development workshop adjacent to the motor bay.

"CZSK P64 pistol," Franz started without a hello. He continued the equipment description in his thick accent. "Polish police izzue, all-zo used by zeir zecret zervice. It fires nine-millimeter Makarov rounds, easily purchased on...

that side, although, Gott help you if you need to. It holds zix rounds in der magazine und one in ze chamber. Over here est your chariot." Franz led Luke to the motor bay.

"Citroen, Jaguar, or maybe an Aston Martin, perhaps?" Luke joked.

"Even better, FNG." Franz smiled as he yanked the cover off Luke's new ride. "A 1968 Yugo, vhite and rust custom paint job."

"What the hell, man? Is this thing even going to make it over there?" demanded Luke. He thought this surely was a joke set up by the guys at the office. After all, Franz knew to call him FNG. "This thing's going to get me killed before I get to the border."

"Appearances can be deceiving, junge. Ve outfitted ze vehicle mit a BMW engine, rebuilt drive train und all new electrical harnezzes. Ze gearbox came from Fiat. It only looks like shit. Ve vant everything back. Ve vorked hard on obtaining these items und dey vere bought by your taxpayer. Vee vant everything back! Unterstand, FNG?"

"All right, I get it: bring everything back," Luke said in a huff. While he was not experienced enough to give Franz any guff, he was tired and nervous about the mission. He began to display outbursts of anger and excitement.

Luke hopped into the Yugo and headed back to NT. Mike was outside smoking a cigarette when he pulled back into the office. "Franz sure has a sense of humor, doesn't he?" Mike asked with a smirk. Luke gave him an inappropriate look. "John's upstairs waiting for you. Remember, follow your training, don't be a hero, and get the job done. We'll have a drink waiting for you."

Luke got upstairs and saw John smoking like a chimney, papers surrounding his desk, and he looked like he hadn't slept in a week. "I just got off the phone with HQ. They want you to go over tonight. Remember your training."

"Let's get this show on the road, John," said Luke.

It was eight o'clock when the guys gave Luke a pat on the back. "Remember your training," said Mike.

"You'll be all right, kid. Just get the job done and we'll see you in a day or so," said Dave.

"No fuckin' around. Get in, get the source, get out. That simple," said John as he shook Luke's hand. Luke could tell that John did not feel comfortable with what he was doing, or what HQ had ordered. But as a soldier, John followed orders, even when he didn't like the potential outcome.

Luke began down the alleyway to take a main thoroughfare to a grand road, and through a series of turns make his way over Glienicke Bridge into the Soviet sector. Luke knew this as the same bridge used to swap Francis Gary Powers and Rudolf Abel in 1962. Thinking through these facts calmed him a bit, but he was still nervous—nervous and calm, an odd combination. But then again, he'd never done anything quite in-depth like this. He knew what was at risk if he got caught. He recalled his training at the Schoolhouse. If he got caught, he would talk; everyone talks. The key was to hold out for as long as possible, so your buddies and sources could get out alive: self-sacrifice or, as he thought of it, martyrdom. "Why should everyone die for you getting caught?" was his philosophy.

Luke arrived at the checkpoint and waited in the queue of automobiles, although they didn't look as bad as his Yugo. Luke prepared his paperwork to make a smooth transition over the border. His palms were dry, but he could feel a cold sweat about to break out. "Stick to the story," he thought. "They don't know what I'm really doing here. Hell, they think everyone is a spy. Just stick to the story. Just *stick* to the *story, just stick to the sto...*" The sound of a horn interrupted his thought. Luke looked up to see a large gap between him and the vehicle in front of him. As he refocused his mind, his hand became steady and he worried what the lack of awareness looked like to the checkpoint guards. Was this common? Would they question him harder? How many other people got distracted looking for their papers? It had to be common.

Luke moved up and was summoned by a guard. As the German sentry looked into the vehicle, he noticed the West German registration sticker on the windscreen. He assumed Luke would be American, given his Western style of haircut. It was longer than a military fade but was no Flock of Seagulls haircut, either. Taking a chance he was right, the guard bellowed "Papers!" to Luke. Luke handed over the documents set up by the agency. "Vat es you biz-ness here?"

Luke could feel the heat intensifying between his lower back and the cheap seats in his Yugo. "I'm a mechanical engineer," Luke got out, followed by a hard, dry swallow.

"Vat biz-ness doos a mechaniker engineer have en East Germany? Ve have our own, better engineer," the guard stated matter-of-factly, with a bit of a grin breaking out. Was he pleased with East Germany's engineers, or was he joking?

The heat in Luke's lower back and armpits intensified. "My business is east of Berlin in a Trabant development and research factory, for export to the West. Your engineers may be better, but our standards are higher."

The East German guard stared Luke down. Luke could tell the guard wanted to lecture him on the evils of capitalism, but that was not his job. The guard looked at the vehicle's exterior, peered through a rear window into the back seat, and quickly handed Luke the papers.

"Enjoy your stay en East Berlin, Mein Herr," the guard said, still staring Luke down. Luke visibly sank in his seat as a sigh of relief escaped his lips. A nervous smile broke out on his face and he took the papers back. Luke thought the story was so obscure as to surely get him caught, but he trusted the guys in the office when they briefed it. Now he knew why. Emotions are a powerful tool to throw people off their original intentions. The crack he made about the West having higher standards was true, but it also wasn't enough of an insult to arouse suspicion or get him detained.

Luke drove to the safe house and met Ingrid, the caretaker, around the corner, a safe distance from the apartment Americans had paid for. After a brief, terse exchange of the types of smoking tobacco available in East Germany, they confirmed each other was who they should be. She was a bit concerned Luke showed up and not John or Dave, the usual agents she met with. She escorted him to the safe house and began to brief Luke on the current Soviet security measures, which ostensibly had to do with John or Dave not being there to meet her.

"The Soviets have been moving around Berlin. Signals intelligence has been worried because they haven't heard much on their front, but human intelligence shows Ivan has taken out two sources without notice," Ingrid explained with a slight accent. Both of these intelligence-collection platforms were vital to create a better picture of any sensitive situation the United States was working on in Berlin. The human intelligence reports Luke had worked with dealt with what people—or more specifically, sources—had seen or heard and then reported back to one of the guys at NT. The signals intelligence allowed for confirmation of information, mostly through electronic readings. Instruments such as a seismometer, normally used to detect earthquakes, could be used to determine if the Soviets were moving tanks or tracked artillery pieces into strategic positions. Information like this corroborated each other independently and then went into supplemental reports like the ones Luke had been poring over for the last few weeks back at the office.

"There has been talk of a double agent in your organization, but your bosses won't entertain the idea someone they allowed to be recruited as being a possible spy."

Ingrid was scared, even though she tried not to show it. It was the way she smoked her cigarette that tipped Luke off and unnerved him. She had to strike the match twice to light it, she took very little time between drags, and her hand was visibly shaking. She changed her arms from being at her sides to her pockets to brushing away errant hairs to tapping on her cigarette to release the ash and back again in a loop.

"There was brief talk about another tunnel that was discovered, but then they went silent." Luke stole one of Ingrid's cigarettes and lit it as he listened. He didn't normally smoke but felt the situation warranted it. He didn't inhale but rather invited the smoke into his mouth and blew it out, much like smoking a cigar. Somehow, the mirroring of Ingrid's body language seemed to calm down her fidgeting. "Security at Checkpoint Charlie has been relaxed to let Westerners in and put a tail on them. At the same time, there has been an increase of that surveillance, harassing anyone who comes through in newer vehicles."

"What about other checkpoints?" Luke calmly asked. He didn't want to disclose he had used another checkpoint to cross over. Ingrid explained how Checkpoint Charlie was the busiest but others would be surveilled from time to time.

It suddenly hit Luke why he was issued a Yugo with a white-and-rust custom paint job. Because it was a popular car in the Soviet Bloc countries, it would mix in with the vehicles parked on the street. The rust on the usual spots of the fenders and doors would show some age, giving it, and the driver, some credibility that they fit in to their surroundings.

Ingrid seemed to relax a bit as she busied herself with cooking dinner. At university she studied Parisian culinary arts, and it showed when she made Luke dinner: steak tartare with french fries cooked in duck fat. Luke had something similar once at a private dinner in college for the International Union of Students.

Luke set out after dinner to contact the Mechanic. Luke drove a good countersurveillance route, or at least what he thought was a good one; he didn't see anyone following him. Dave's advice helped make the route seem like a normal drive about the city if he were being surveilled. Luke was really attempting to force the Soviet surveillance team, if there was one, to appear behind him several times in different parts of the city so he could make a decision on whether to proceed to his final destination. Most businesses were closed, so stopping and pulling additional countersurveillance on foot was difficult. After determining he was free of any Soviet surveillance, Luke parked and walked two blocks to the cabstand, where he met the Mechanic. As he approached, Luke saw a man fifty meters from the cabstand smoking a cigarette.

"Are those Turkish tobacco, by chance?" asked Luke.

"They are, but I prefer American," the Mechanic said.

"I find Turkish are better quality," Luke responded. Just as he had rehearsed with Mike.

The Mechanic threw his cigarette in the gutter and took Luke's arm. "Come with me; there's no time to waste." The Mechanic took Luke to the back of the cabstand. They began a slow jog through back alleys and ducked into a small apartment. This place looked like the stuff nightmares were made of: cockroaches everywhere, a sink full of dishes with half-eaten meals still rotting, and a dirty, crude wooden table with what looked like dried blood on it.

"I've been followed for the last week. Someone gave me up. I can't do this anymore. *You* need to get me out. *Now, tonight!*"

"Calm down, take a breath, and think," Luke said. "Is anyone in immediate danger to your knowledge?" The Mechanic fervently shook his head no. "What makes you think you're in danger?" Luke asked.

"The Soviets have been taking people out, sending them to the Gulag, holding summary trials, and executing people for nonexistent crimes. They took in three of my men. I don't have any way of getting you the information requested."

"That's why I'm here. I'm going to get you out of here," Luke assured him. "But we can't leave right away. I just came over the border a few hours ago. We know the same men will be on the checkpoint. It's too risky to leave now."

"But we need to go now! I need to get the hell out of here!" yelled the Mechanic.

"I can't just drive over the border with a West German in the car like a tourist trip, not at this hour. We need to think this through and figure out why you're leaving your country," Luke tried to reason.

"This isn't my country; I have no allegiance to the fucking Nazis or the Soviets or the Americans or the bloody British. At this point my loyalty is to myself and my family."

Suddenly the door violently opened and three men came rushing in. No words were said, just action. Luke and the Mechanic were tackled to the ground. One man began his best efforts to drive his fist straight through the Mechanic's face and cracked the floorboards underneath. Luke felt the sharp crack of cold steel against his neck. Another blow was delivered to Luke's head and he felt the cold embrace of darkness and defeat.

Luke came to tied to a chair, naked, in a cold room. It was like a jail cell mixed with an office.

While there was a light, it was in poor working order, effectively shining light on a thin sliver of the room, leaving the corners darkened. Poor ventilation and water damage must have contributed to the musty odor Luke smelled. There were bars on the one-foot-by-one-foot black-painted window, and Luke made out a desk in the corner with an audio recorder. The entrance was a heavy industrial steel door; there was enough ambient light reflected off it to shine some light in that section of the room. The door had obviously been replaced at least once, and there were dents in the door at the same height of an average man sitting in a chair. The door opened and a Russian major walked in.

The major was tall and fit. He appeared middle-aged, but the salt-and-pepper hair he had on the sides of his balding head made him appear a bit older. Luke knew the major was in his field uniform because of the lack of cords and medals hanging from his shirt. The uniform materials looked new, not surprising for Russian officers stationed in East Germany. Russians who would interact with the outside world were given all new equipment and uniforms for the same reason they were given better food: the government wanted to portray a better society, even if the whole system was just painted rust. If weak, emaciated soldiers in tattered uniforms were seen across the fence from Western journalists, surely there would be questions about the system that took care of them and whether the rest of the world should follow for the pursuit of a "just society."

The major removed his service cap and placed it in the waist pocket of his long, gray wool coat. Luke thought it odd to have so many heavy layers on when it was still early in the fall season, even for Germany. The four shiny buttons were undone with some difficulty, demonstrating how new the coat was. The major removed the coat and threw it over the chair. He removed a pack of Lucky Strike cigarettes from his hip pocket and placed them on the edge of the desk. Although he was about to extol the virtues of Communism to Luke, he certainly did take advantage of the black market made available with the help of capitalist intent.

"It would seem we have a dilemma here. My superiors want you hanged as a spy publicly, where the West can see your dangling body." The major cleared his throat as a soldier walked into the room with water, two glasses, and a stack of documents. The major dismissed the soldier and filled one glass halfway, taking a drink. "You arrived in West Berlin three weeks ago, assigned to the Nähere Telekommunikation front business, and own the shitty Yugo parked three blocks from where we found you."

Luke had let his imagination run wild before the mission with the worst-case scenarios. He wasn't far off the mark. Would this be the first interrogation of many? If the major already knew about him, what was there to discuss? Other than the blow to the back of the head when they picked him up, there had been no further physical inflictions to him.

The major went on. "You Americans thought you were clever, filling in your spy tunnels with wood and crates to make us think there was nothing there."

"How does he know that information?" Luke thought. Did someone give up NT, the tunnel operations, the logistics support team, and their gadgets? How much did the Mechanic know? How much was he able to tell them? Luke sat quietly, looking up at the major sheepishly.

The major took a short breath in and rolled his eyes from the upper right to upper left corner before speaking. "You may believe capitalism will win, but even your own nation doesn't believe that. Your military was superior, but the heroic peoples of Vietnam took down the mighty giant. No matter how much money your capitalist government threw at the war in Vietnam, the ideals of equality and justice won the people. Communism has won in Vietnam, and socialism is winning in your country as well. Your college students are enlightened to the ways of socialism and how much better it is for society. They will come around to the good of Communism as well. Why can you not understand this? Why can your government not understand this?"

Luke knew the major was just saying these things to soften him up to the idea of utter defeat. If he was brainwashed to the ways of Communism like so many other people around the world, he might turn and give up information. But if the major already knew so much about the tunnels and who Luke was, then why would he need any more information on the same subjects?

Luke's mind wandered to the summers he had spent earning merit badges in Boy Scouts and practices with his football team. He thought of the guys in the office and whether they would be disappointed with his being caught.

The major put a map in front of Luke. "Show me where the other tunnels are located."

Luke looked at the major and began to explain. "You know who I am, what I drive, and where I was tonight. You even said I have been in Germany for three weeks. Why would I know such vital information after such a short time being here?" Luke stopped and thought of his next words carefully. "I cannot help you, Major."

The major checked his wristwatch, cleared his throat, and turned out of the room. "We will speak again when you are ready." Two soldiers entered the room, one with a brown cloth roll with something heavy inside. One soldier cleared the desk while the other unrolled the cloth. Luke didn't know what they had, but it radiated the little light the room had to offer like the chrome of surgical instruments.

Chapter 6

Exceeding Efforts

Luke looked like a shipwreck survivor as he shuffled from the back of an East German military truck with the major and two Russian soldiers escorting him to the American sector of West Berlin. The United States had agreed to hand over an Italian woman convicted of spying through a young marine stationed at the embassy. It had been three weeks since Luke was taken by the Russians. They kept him alive but just barely. His meals were not appetizing but had enough nutrients to keep him from starving. The little water he was given by his captors was dirty and had a metallic odor to it, but it kept him from dying of dehydration. The pants of the oversized blue-and-white-striped pajamas he was given kept getting caught under his feet as he walked toward freedom. Luke shuffled along in the oversized, tattered leather shoes given to him when his shoes were deemed "too nice for him." An old Russian Army coat provided enough warmth in the mid-fall early morning air. It kept the light rain from penetrating down to his bones. The short beard on his neck and face also helped keep some body heat trapped next to his skin.

"It looks like I was right, spy. You were more useful to us alive. Do not look upon the heroes of the Motherland when you pass them. And don't think of attempting any retribution; the whole world is watching this exchange."

The Soviets had brought a photographer along to document the exchange; most likely they would turn it into propaganda against the West. The United States had a representative of every intelligence organization hidden along the tall buildings surrounding the small checkpoint with cameras; they wanted faces and body language. The world would not see their photographs.

East German and Russian guards in new uniforms lined the widened area used for vehicle searches on the Soviet side of the checkpoint. They too were there for propaganda purposes. They were also there to try to scare the West from attempting to send their spies into Soviet territory. They also aided in psychologically aiding released spies to give up their profession.

But all Luke could think about was getting back to the West, eating solid, edible food with a cold beer, followed by a hot shower, and sleeping in an actual bed for hours upon hours. He could see John on the other side of the checkpoint smoking like a chimney, pacing back and forth waiting for Luke to stumble through so he could be greeted and debriefed.

"You look great, Luke" John said. "We understand you've been through some traumatic stuff, but we do need to sit down with you and debrief any information you may have, no matter how trivial. Take the night. Eat, shower, sleep. Enjoy yourself, Luke. Tomorrow we'll sit down and talk."

Luke felt relieved to know there was a plan in place, especially since it allowed him to get all the things he had been dreaming about doing for the past few days since hearing the news of his spy swap.

"We have a hotel room for you; your quarters were packed up—" John stopped midsentence, suddenly catching himself. "Just in case..."

"Say no more; I understand. You followed protocol," said Luke.

The convoy whisked them away, and Luke felt relief. Relief for his freedom, relief not to have to worry about the late-night calls from the major, relief in knowing he was safe again.

"How are you holding up, Luke?" asked John. "Is this still the line of work you want?"

"I thought debrief didn't start until tomorrow morning, John," Luke stated.

"Very good, Luke. Very good. I guess that's what we get for hiring a kid with a master's degree."

"Even after all I've been through, you're gonna break my stones?"

The next morning came too fast for Luke. He had a great night's sleep and even better dinner. He put on his suit, which was a little too big due to the weight he had lost over three weeks of captivity, and headed downstairs to the lobby for his ride to the office. Dave showed up looking a little hung over.

"You look like shit, kid," Dave blurted out. Tact was not Dave's strong suit.

"It's good to see you too, killer," Luke fired back as he moved in for a hug.

"We're all really glad to have you back, kid." They got into the car and zoomed off through morning traffic. "I'm sure you're wondering about your future in fieldwork." It was an uncomfortable topic, but Luke was curious about his future in counterespionage. There were other assignments available to counterespionage agents, but no one wanted them. Field operations were the pinnacle of skill sets for agents to use. Many went their whole career without running sources, and Luke was put into the position immediately. Good timing and a bit of luck got him there.

"There's been word of sending you to work at G2-Special Branch over in Bamberg," Dave said. The Special Branch office dealt with human intelligence, counterespionage, and Black Ops projects. It was an administrative section overseeing reports, legal authorities, and personnel management of field collectors. It came with lots of recognition from the top brass but little satisfaction from those who worked there.

"Given your talents in analytics and report writing in the Schoolhouse, you can still be in the fight, just not over the East/West line. Sorry, kid; we're all burned. There's talk of having the entire North American enterprise flip-flop with us in Europe. It's the only way to continue collecting over the Wall. But there has been an order halting all operations until you came back. I guess we'll just have to wait and see."

All these changes were not what Luke wanted to hear, but he had a strong suspicion it was coming. They arrived at the office and went to the back. Mike and Willy were there and expressed their sympathies for what had happened. Willy summoned Luke to the interview room, where they could conduct a debrief of what Luke had observed. Or gave up under interrogation.

"If any of this upsets you, feel free to take a break, kid," Willy started. "So let's start from the beginning: the afternoon you left here to go over the line."

"I drove through with no issues. As I continued through, I began my surveillance route from the checkpoint on the bridge. Not too many establishments were open at 1700 on a Sunday, so I stopped at a café, took in a scone and cappuccino. I was there for about fifteen minutes before making my way through the north side of the city, where I stopped at a chemist for cough syrup, as the trip over triggered my allergies. I drove around taking a series of turns to the stopping point. I parked about two blocks away and transitioned on foot to the final stop, the cabstand. The trip took about ninety minutes."

He continued, "I went to the first safe-house location meeting site. Ingrid was there. We went to the authorized apartment and she briefed me on what was going on. She was scared but tried not to show it. I'm sure she had her theories on who the mole was… is," Luke corrected himself. "She warned me not to go, but I knew I had to complete my mission."

"Did you meet the Mechanic?" Willy asked.

"I went through another route, just to make sure I was clean. After what Ingrid told me, I wanted to be cautious. I drove for another forty minutes before making it to the meeting site. The Mechanic was on the spot described in the dossier, smoking, so I approached and initiated the bona fides. He responded correctly, and he took me through a series of alleyways to a safe site."

"Whose safe site? Was this location in any of the dossier?" Willy asked excitedly.

"No, I wasn't aware of this site. And it all happened very fast. I couldn't point it out, exactly. But I know it wasn't an authorized safe house."

"What happened next?" Mike asked calmly.

"He was spooked about something, so I rerecruited him due to his hesitancy to stay in the operation. He stated his sub-sources were killed or imprisoned and he didn't want that to happen to him. He demanded exfiltration to the West immediately. He demanded we hop in the Trabant and go over to the East that minute. He was pretty rattled."

"Was there any indication he was dirty? Any signal or indication you were gonna get rolled up?" Willy immediately regretted using the term "rolled up," but he was searching for any tell the Mechanic was a double agent. Did he sell out his handler? Was he followed at some point that night? Did one of his sub-sources give up everything?

"He seemed genuine. I have no reason to believe he was a double," Luke defended. "He seemed really spooked about the whole affair," Luke stated again for emphasis.

"What happened when you discussed exfiltrating him?" Mike asked as he reached for a pack of cigarettes.

"He told me everyone in his network was getting nabbed by the Stasi. That's when it happened…" Luke stopped to get a cup of coffee from the breakroom before going on with the debrief. He came back in the room and stood in the corner as he continued.

"Three men in black suits broke down the door. We were rolled up and I don't know what happened to the Mechanic. I think he's dead, but I have nothing to base that on."

"Where were you taken?" Willy inquired.

"I don't know. I felt a blow from something to the back of my head and woke up in an office–interrogation room." Luke recalled the event as he reached for the base of his skull. It hurt just thinking about it.

"Who handled you when you were over there?"

"A major. Athletic build, with a short, Caesar haircut, and he didn't smoke. His English was clean with a British accent on certain words," Luke said with his voice beginning to shake.

"And what kind of questions did he ask?" Willy pressed on, attempting to understand what, if anything, Luke had given up.

"He asked about the Mechanic. He was pressing me for their operations and how we recruited him, who he and his sub-sources passed information to, who they were collecting on for us. I think he already knew but wanted me to confirm their intelligence."

The debriefing took two hours. Luke felt like he was run through the wringer with Willy. He was trained on debriefing techniques but was no expert. Willy had been doing this for twenty years and left no stone unturned. Luke was finally let go to take care of some administrative tasks before knocking off early.

John summoned Luke into his office after lunch and confirmed he was being reassigned, if he still wanted to stay in Germany, to Bamberg, G2-Special Branch. Luke accepted the position. He loved the job so far and wanted to see where this path took him.

That night was like his first in the apartment—just the furniture that came with the place, Mike and Dave coming over to have a few drinks more than they already had. John had arranged for Luke's possessions to be shipped back from the storage facility after they got word of his impending release. There was no use unpacking after the news he had gotten earlier that day.

"Is there any ice in the fridge?" asked Dave as he made his way back to the kitchen. Mike melted into the same seat he took that first night, drink already in hand. Dave came back from the kitchen with two drinks, handing one to Luke.

"Tough break, kid. But at least you're still alive. You should quit the game and write a book!" Dave tried his best to keep his faux pas to a minimum when he talked to Luke about his future. "Did you get orders for your new office job?"

"No, I have to go in tomorrow and talk to the ladies at the front for personnel transfers. They should be cut by Thursday; I leave Friday, have the weekend to get settled in to the city, and go to work on Monday." Luke described the process quietly, hanging his head with a bit of shame. Maybe it was the shame of getting caught, maybe because he felt like he had let the team down.

"Well, at least we have three more nights with you. Cheers, fellas! Welcome back, Luke." Mike raised his glass in the air; Dave and Luke raised theirs. A solemn moment filled the room before they all took a drink.

A week later Luke arrived at Bamberg Army Complex and reported to Lieutenant Colonel Smith. "Welcome to Bamberg, Luke. I heard what happened and how skilled you are. Let us know if there's anything you need. I'm placing you in the G2-Special Branch section in charge of source management. Take a good look at the existing dossiers to determine if there are any insider threats: doubles, dangles, high-threat persons who possess qualities to make them flip. Considering events of the recent weeks, we need to assure Washington, D.C., our operations are sound."

"I fully understand, sir. I'm excited to get to work," Luke said enthusiastically.

Chapter 7

A Fresh Start

Luke was shown to his new office after his meeting with Lieutenant Colonel Smith. It was small but made even smaller by all the filing cabinets along the walls to his left and right. They held source dossiers, code names and numbers for future operations, and dead files from previous sources who had either defected or gotten killed. The desk had a computer caked with dust; apparently his predecessor had failed to clean in his time there. Coffee stains in the form of endless Venn diagrams tattooed the left side of the desk. The right side had indentations where someone had been taking notes on a couple pieces of paper or less; some words could still be made out. Luke was torn on whether to clean the coffee stains, as he was right-handed too and would eventually add to the mess. In the end he decided to clean the stains. Besides, walking around the office would allow him to get to know his coworkers and the facilities.

Luke squeezed through the small space between the end of his new desk and one of the filing cabinets toward the door and into the hallway. He walked toward the open production floor where all the analysts worked, stopped, looked around, and decided to go toward the far end of the room, where some soldiers were hanging out by the coffee machine.

As Luke turned, he was hit suddenly by a flurry of camouflage and paperwork. "I am so sorry! I didn't see you there! Gosh, I am such a klutz." Her name was Sarah, an army enlisted analyst and go-fer around the office. She had her long black hair in a bun except for a slim ribbon that had come loose after running into Luke that framed the left side of her plain face.

"Here, let me help you with your files, miss," Luke said as he bent down to aid in collecting the manila envelopes that covered the tile floor like carpet. Luke's training took over and he began to assess Sarah. She wasn't wearing a wedding ring, nor was there a tan line or indent where one might be. Her alabaster skin and thin frame made Luke wonder if she could meet the physical fitness standards of the army.

"Hi, my name is... ah... Sarah!" she stammered out as she made eye contact with Luke. As she took him in, she tilted her head with a nervous smile and asked Luke his name. Luke introduced himself as he handed the files back.

"I'm Luke; I just transferred here. Do you know where I can get cleaning supplies?" While Luke had a suspicion Sarah might be infatuated with him, he just wanted to get into the files in his office.

"Yeah, I can show you!" Sarah let out like she was leading a cop to the scene of a crime. The discovery of a lifetime for Sarah was showing the new guy where the janitor's closet was. Luke wondered what her standing was with the rest of the analysts and got his answer shortly. As they walked past the coffee station, the rest of the analysts gave her a disapproving glare. They didn't even see Luke.

"Here it is, for all your janitorial needs!" Sarah joked to Luke. He feigned a courtesy laugh and thanked her for her help. As he reached for the supplies, he thought of an easy, quick way out of a potentially awkward situation.

"Thanks for the help. I hope I have enough time to clean before my meeting. What time is it?" Luke looked at his watch to prevent her from answering. "Oh, crap! I have to go!" Sarah looked disappointed as Luke thanked her again and walked off briskly back to his office.

Luke closed his office door, put the cleaning supplies on top of a filing cabinet, and dove into the files. He spent countless hours shuffling through his predecessor's work, trying to piece together everything, destroying unnecessary documents and multiple copies. When he felt frustrated or tired of looking at dossiers, he would get some cleaning done.

"What are you still doing here, Luke?" LTC Smith asked. It was 2200 and everyone had left for the day except Smith and his aide. Smith's sudden presence startled Luke.

"Sir, oh, I was shuffling through the files, getting them organized before I can start systematically scrubbing them for those indicators you wanted me to look for in each of the sources to see if there's any indicators of..."

"Fine, fine, Luke. You did just get here, and the previous seat-holder sucked something fierce. I'm not saying take your time, but don't stand on your head trying to take on a task so involved," LTC Smith instructed. "You have been through a traumatic event, Luke. It's all right to take a step back and breathe a little. Find yourself a girl; go explore the city." After Smith's friendly advice, Luke thought back to John challenging him with the girl in the café.

"Yes, sir. I'll take that advice, sir," Luke said with a smirk.

LTC Smith gave Luke a look. "Have a good night, Luke."

LTC Smith thought it a bit odd that Luke, being so young, would have such a hard work ethic and wondered if he was just suppressing what had happened to him by working through the mental duress.

As the weeks passed, Luke kept plugging away at his work. He didn't particularly enjoy the company of those who worked at the G2 Intelligence Office. They were office drones, he thought. They didn't understand anything outside their little windowless world and the office politics that allowed everything to run smoothly.

Every Friday the office would go to lunch just outside the base for German Friday. It was a way of relaxing and gaining esprit de corps for the mandatory life everyone had signed up for with their military contracts.

"Are you coming to lunch?" Sarah asked, as she stuck her head into Luke's office, unsolicited.

A Fresh Start | 113

Luke tried his best to avoid the German Fridays and had been successful so far. But he was unprepared when Sarah barged into his office. Luke thought for a moment to search for a credible lie but gave in. He understood the office politics and was quite aware of the need to socialize with these people if he were to make the best of everyday life here.

"Yeah, sure. Why not? Are we going to the Italian joint again?" Luke joked. He knew sporadic activities with his coworkers was a good compromise to prevent hanging out with them at night and on weekends.

As the group walked out for lunch, Luke saw through LTC Smith's cracked-open door that he was on the phone.

"So how is he adjusting, Kevin?" John asked LTC Smith on their weekly phone call.

"He seemed to have a hard time at first—working long hours, not going out with the office, just not letting people into his life, really. But he seems to be coming around." LTC Smith was making the statement as he observed Luke walk out with the rest of the office for the first time since he had been reassigned. "In the last two years he's gone from graduate school to training to you guys to their guys to us. It's quite an adjustment, and he's still too inexperienced to know what the world is made of."

As LTC Smith continued his phone call with John, the office was just sitting down to eat at the German sausage restaurant around the corner from the main gate of post. As everyone settled in, awaiting their meals, the usual small talk ensued.

"I'm glad you came out to lunch with all of us, Luke," Sarah exclaimed as she attempted to gain all of Luke's attention. "So what unit were you with before Bamberg?"

"I was at an investigative unit."

"I don't quite know what you mean. Were you an internal affairs soldier?" Sarah asked. Of course, she would ask something like that; it seemed to Luke the other intelligence disciplines didn't know or understand what counterespionage did or how it affected their mission.

"I would investigate spies wherever they may be throughout the Department of Defense, with particular emphasis on contractors and soldiers who went over the line frequently." This was the standard line they gave people in casual conversation to baffle them and get them to change the topic.

"That sounds… interesting," Sarah shyly retorted. "What do you like to do when you're off duty?" The sudden change of topic meant the standard answer about investigations had worked.

The usual banter happened throughout the meal, like office talk, unclassified and nonsensical to the bystander, of course, while the men would talk about football and the women talked about sites they would like to visit while on a free European vacation courtesy of Uncle Sam. Luke, however, constantly checked his watch.

"Do you have somewhere to be?" Sarah inquired.

"I believe in taking no longer than necessary during lunch to maximize my workday," Luke stated matter-of-factly.

Luke waved down the waitress and paid his bill in a hurried manner. "I'll see you all back in the office."

Sarah's disappointment at Luke's departure was noticeable. "I'll... we'll see you back there, Luke," she said.

LTC Smith was finishing his weekly phone call with John as the group came stumbling back into the office thirty minutes late. It was apparent they, or at least some, had been drinking. Smith didn't mind, as it was Friday and they all seemed to have their faculties.

"Where's Luke, Sarah?" She explained to Smith how Luke had left the group to return to work about fifty minutes earlier. Just then he came strolling around the corner with a dossier under his arm.

"Where have you been, Luke?" Smith asked. "Archives, sir; just fact-checking some items from a current operation with a past one." LTC

Smith couldn't remember seeing Luke pass by his large office window in the past hour, but then again, maybe he didn't have to. Luke probably just went straight to archives and had been there since.

"If you have a moment, sir..." Luke requested as he motioned with his hand to LTC Smith's office. As Luke closed the office door, Smith knew he had something, or at least hoped he did. Luke had been burning the midnight oil since he arrived, and LTC Smith was worried Luke was going to burn out.

"I've been looking over the files, sir, and think there may be a double in our organization." This statement made LTC Smith worried; burnout was one thing, paranoia was another. Luke had been assigned to Bamberg only a month and he was coming forward with a double-agent threat. How could he have figured something like that out so fast?

"I was looking through the historic files and noted an Agent Williams, Mitch Williams, who is on his fourth tour; that's eight years," Luke exclaimed, almost tripping over his words.

"Where's the part why I should care, Luke?" Smith sighed out.

"Williams is single, lives a lavish lifestyle, and has been running a female source for six years. His source reports are lacking and don't match with the dates of his intelligence reports where he allegedly met with her."

"OK," LTC Smith began. "So Williams is homesteading. Maybe he likes being in Europe. He's running a female source. Many agents run female sources; it doesn't mean they're sleeping with them. And so what if he's single? Maybe that gives him a leg up. Or maybe he's just bad with women. We don't know what his personal preferences are.

"But, sir..." Luke interrupted.

"You need to remember where you stand on this team, Agent!" LTC Smith raised his voice at Luke. "However," Smith continued, "you do have a compelling argument for a second look of Agent Williams. As I recall he was assigned here to conduct counterespionage analytics after the incident that took you down." LTC Smith stopped himself from going further into such a traumatic event. "Many agents were compromised, so there was a lot of shuffling afterward. He has always been described as a good agent. But if these reports are lacking, and any of them pertain to the mission you were on, then it may be worth another look. Tread carefully, Luke. Williams has a clean record; obtain the facts before rushing to judgment." LTC Smith was cautious but allowed Luke to take a closer look at Agent Williams's files and assessments of his source, as well as any intelligence reporting he turned in.

"Thank you, sir. Thank you very much, sir," Luke groveled as he backed away from LTC Smith's desk and out the door.

"That sounded a bit heated," Sarah said to Luke as he bumped into her. She had her trademark manila files clutched to her chest.

"Yeah, I guess I got a bit ahead of myself."

"Need any help?" Sarah offered. At first Luke wanted to walk away as fast as he could without answering her but thought about her offer for a moment. It occurred to Luke there were aspects of the office he was unwilling, or unable, to comprehend. Sarah had been in Bamberg for three years as an intelligence analyst. She must have read some of Williams's reports.

"As a matter of fact, Sarah, there are some things you can help with. Once I get some info stripped out, I'll call you into a special project I'm working on."

"That's the first time you called me by my first name," Sarah squealed.

"I wasn't sure I could get away with it," replied Luke with a smirk. "What do you know about Agent Williams?"

"Oh, he's one of the best agents around. He's been doing this so long he must have written the manual on whatever it is you do in the field. But I'm sure you're better... Luke." Sarah called Luke by his first name to reciprocate the familiarity.

"I'll meet with you tomorrow and discuss any requirements we need your expertise on." Luke hesitated momentarily before taking a casual seat on the nearby desk. "You do understand this task will require the utmost discretion. Can I trust your confidence on this matter, Sarah?"

Sarah squeaked out a "Yup" as she violently nodded her head up and down and simultaneously turned three shades of red.

"Excellent! So I'll see you tomorrow, about 1000 hours?" Luke confirmed. Sarah just nodded her head faster and clutched her files closer to her chest before scurrying away back to her desk.

Chapter 8

The Hunt

"Good morning! I hope you're ready to work on this project" Luke shot to Sarah before she could return the salutation. "I need to know anything and everything about the Baker and Agent Williams. Remember, this is being done in total secrecy; not a word to anyone. There's special interest in his intelligence reports and any files pertaining to his interactions with the Baker."

"I'll bring them right up," Sarah assured with her most professional demeanor.

"Let's not work on this here. You still need to complete your assignments during the duty day. We'll meet up at my place on Eins Strasse, the new apartment complex. Do you know it?"

Sarah returned to those three shades of red she had displayed the previous night. "Yeah, I'm familiar with them," Sarah let out with restraint to her excitement. "Should I come in uniform?"

"Come however you feel comfortable, but preferably not in a uniform," Luke said with a crooked smirk. "Just put the files into a manila envelope when you leave the office; don't put a classification cover sheet on it. Meet at my place after work, say 5:30?" Luke changed from the twenty-four-hour clock to the twelve-hour clock in order to see how well she would adjust to the change of vernacular. Luke wanted her to appear less military in her speech and mannerisms.

"I'll be there with bells on, Luke," she said with an awkward, flirty smirk and half wink.

"You need to be aware of the importance of these investigations. It's paramount to carry on like we're not investigating one of our own. The gathering of files, and research, even the safeguarding of the aggregate information we find, will be a slow and arduous process. We will have to work long hours and hide things from everyone else, even if it doesn't seem right, even if the person you're talking to outranks you, even if the person is someone you consider a friend; this operation needs to be kept secret. Do you understand, Sarah?"

There was no color change from Sarah this time. In fact, there was no color at all. She was white as a ghost. "I understand and will do anything that's necessary to aid you in this task," she said quietly with dedication and confidence in her voice. Even though Luke was shuffling some files on his desk, she continued to look at him with awe and respect. Luke was so calm in his demeanor, as if he didn't have a personal stake in what the investigation might reveal.

Sarah carried out her tasks, both assigned and given in secret, throughout the day. She showed up to Luke's apartment at 5:20 and waited patiently until 5:25 before knocking loud three times on the door. Luke opened the door about halfway.

"I have what you need," she said in a low voice.

"Why don't you come in so we can speak freely?" Luke offered as he opened the door all the way to usher her in. Luke had a bottle of wine out and offered a glass to Sarah. "I'll look over these in time." Luke threw the files onto his small dining table behind him and closed the door. Luke and Sarah did not get to the files that night.

Over the next three weeks, Sarah did what Luke instructed on their fateful night at his apartment and acted in the same manner she did since before Luke had arrived at Bamberg. She continued her interactions with her colleagues during the day and would meet with Luke three nights a week. Luke had hit a point in the investigation where he needed more information than the files could tell him. He summoned Sarah to his office.

"I need your help with something, if you're interested in fieldwork" Luke said as he leaned back in his chair. Sarah nodded her head approvingly but enthusiastically. Luke continued, "I need to know who Williams is meeting with. Are you willing to follow him with me?"

Sarah obliged, of course. She was willing to follow Luke to hell and back, especially after that first night at his apartment. He told her they needed to live two lives, one as professionals at work and another in the shadows, following friends and colleagues. Emotions would collide if the two worlds were to meet, so feelings of distance between them in the office did not mean there were feelings of distance when they were out of the office. Luke assured her there was a need for safety and security in their relationship. Sarah had some concerns, but Luke assured her there was more at stake than just interpersonal feelings; it was the freedom of the whole world, which was represented by the Berlin Wall keeping oppression in and freedom out. Sarah understood what Luke was saying with such conviction before they spent the evening together three weeks prior. Sarah was sure she was doing the right thing aiding Luke in defeating the tyranny of Soviet oppression.

"Tonight I'll teach you what you need to know, and we can move to the next phase of the investigation this weekend. Americans love to party on the weekends, starting Thursday night and ending when they come out of their drunken stupor sometime on Monday morning."

Although they had been meeting after work three times a week, Luke identified a need to train Sarah in the event he needed her to follow someone alone. She also needed to know when she was being followed. Luke took Monday, Tuesday, and Wednesday night to train her in rudimentary tradecraft. The hours were long, and he was tired of looking at maps after using monopoly pieces to represent her, him, and the adversary's agents in possible scenarios.

The weekend came fast for Luke, but it felt like an eternity for Sarah. After their training sessions on maps, walking and driving about the city, and more "private" sessions in Luke's apartment, they set out to follow Agent Williams and see what he was up to. Neither one had ever met Williams face-to-face, although they had heard of his exploits. Sarah read his reports coming out the field, naturally, being an analyst.

"We can pose as a couple to get things rolling; start off at his apartment and see where he goes." Luke had planned everything to keep Sarah slightly unwitting of advanced tradecraft methods. He did have Agent Williams's photo in the car for both to study, including photos at different angles so they could be sure it was him.

"I see him! There!" Sarah exclaimed. "All right, calm down. Describe what he's wearing, what he's doing, and where he's going," Luke advised. The rest of the night went this way—Sarah squealing something out or overcorrecting herself on a previous call about Williams's actions and Luke bringing her back from the edge, trying to keep his calm. They followed him for two weekends starting on Thursdays: They parked outside Williams's apartment, waited until he left, leapfrogged ahead to a local gambling parlor, and hung out in the corner of the bar to watch him lose half his paycheck. Williams headed back home, but not before stopping at a corner store to pick up a pint of ice cream for who appeared to be his girlfriend. Like LTC Smith told Luke when he began the investigation, there was nothing wrong with being single. But Luke knew there were reasons for Americans with security clearances to hide foreign associations. This would be another puzzle piece for Luke to find in the mysterious swamp of facts and fiction.

Saturday and Sunday were reserved for Williams and his girlfriend. They would go to the city center or the art museum or, if one was in town, a fair or carnival. Luke determined Williams's schedule was fairly rigid but wanted to know about the rest of his week. Luke began to follow him on weeknights, alternating days with no particular set schedule. Sometimes he would go alone, other times he had Sarah with him, and on two occasions Luke sent Sarah by herself; she was getting quite good at following Williams. This surveillance lasted fifteen weeks. Months of late nights and boring hours of sitting in a vehicle to figure out what Williams was doing at various locations. But like any other person in any other culture, Williams was a creature of habit. His rigid schedule on the weekends extended to his weekdays. It seems Williams had a young lady he was keeping company on the other side of the city. He was very clever about his affair: he would alternate weekdays once a week and take every sixth week off. After about fifteen weeks, Luke had figured it out—week one: Wednesday night; week two: Monday night; week three: Friday night; week four: Tuesday night; week five: Thursday night; week six: No contact. Williams was very exacting in his schedule. It would have been very difficult to trail him if only he weren't so exacting. Williams was so predictable, Luke and Sarah were able to drop in on him at different places within a five-minute window week after week.

At one point in the surveillance they saw two silhouette cast on the white curtains. One looked like Williams - and the timing to enter the building made sense. Sarah pointed out how the two figures interacted like parents-to-be, and the female outline suggested she was right. While having a child out of wedlock was not illegal for agents, having a child with a foreign national required they be registered on the agent's security clearance. And as far as everyone in the office knew, Williams was single. A one-night stand was not considered continuing contact, so it was overlooked by security. Living with a foreign national needed to be noted, and especially having a child with them. His clearance paperwork was not updated. What was Williams hiding in this relationship? What did he have to gain being in it that he also had to lose admitting he was with her romantically?

After Luke had established a pattern of life for Williams, he and Sarah would repeat the process on different nights, but only once a week. The only thing they didn't know was who his other mistress was: She never came down to greet Williams; he had a key. And she never came to the balcony of her apartment, as she either didn't smoke or smoked indoors. One night, though, the woman left the lights on inside her apartment on a dark evening and got too close to the window; the clear outline of the soft curves of a woman were observed by both Luke and Sarah. Another time Williams had apparently forgotten his key to the apartment and had to ring the buzzer. Sarah went to the buzzer he pressed to look for a name - it was listed as "Occupied" instead of a tenant name. While they were convinced Williams was seeing this woman on the side, Luke needed more evidence of wrongdoing. He was probably a philanderer but was not doing anything illegal. Williams's actions did not match the characteristics of a spy.

"Given the evidence thus far, sir, I need authorization for funding and equipment to prove guilt or innocence of Agent Williams." Luke was firm but respectful as he described the situation to LTC Smith. "We know he's a habitual gambler, and he seems to lose more money than he earns. He has a child on the way; we don't know who the girl is, but she seems to be German. She is not listed on his clearance paperwork. There's also a Jane Doe in the fold. I don't know what, if anything, is going into or out of that apartment."

"So what's your plan, Luke?" Smith asked, sounding half convinced he was on to something. As LTC Smith was listening, he was rubbing his eyes. He had much to worry about as a commander, and the thought that someone in his ranks was spying seemed unlikely to him. But that's what Luke was brought in to do: catch spies.

"I want to rent the apartment across from Jane Doe's complex and outfit it with binoculars, video cameras, and audio surveillance equipment."

"And how much is this going to cost the taxpayers?"

"Sir, my figures so far are $5,000 for the surveillance equipment, 300 Deutsche Marks to get the apartment, and another 175 per month to keep it."

"That's all you're getting, Luke," Smith warned. "If you come back asking for a food stipend, don't."

"Well then, sir, I should also ask for operational funds, in case I find a source who lives in the building. Given the current economic state, I think 1,000 Deutsche Marks available for use should suffice."

LTC Smith let out a forced laugh to tactfully let Luke know his request was beyond realistic. "How about this: I'll approve 500 for now, with another 500 earmarked. But it will only become available after the source's personal information is provided *and* you show what intelligence they've been providing, *and* you provide an assessment of their personality, with all this packaged up neatly and presented to me. Then all of this will go through the psych section as well as a counterintelligence dossier review board. Oh! *And* this will all be done prior to you recruiting them as an official asset of the U.S. government."

A nervous twitch Luke had was slowly coming out. After all the conscious efforts through college to stop himself, he still had it when he felt he was losing control. When he would get anxious or angry, or even just in uncomfortable situations, Luke blinked incessantly and the left corner of his mouth would jerk like he was biting his lip internally. Smith could see the twitch intensify as much as Luke could feel it.

"Yes, sir. I fully understand, sir. I'll get right on the surveillance house and profiling for a suitable source." Luke stuttered as he tried to sound humble through his anger and confusion. Luke thought of LTC Smith as a peer, ignoring the years of military service he had over Luke's graduate degree. Luke realized those years of service were exactly what gave LTC Smith the credibility over Luke's education status. Even with that, Luke was not in the military; he didn't have to take orders from LTC Smith, per se. What had he done that made LTC Smith feel it necessary to correct him? Luke was trained as a counterespionage agent; LTC Smith was not. He was just a generic intelligence officer. Luke failed to understand the nuances of military, and even the civilian sector of the government, pecking order, better known as clout. Just as Luke's twitching came to a crescendo, he knew he would still have to play nice with the military sector, and John would hear any stories about Luke being unruly. John's opinion about Luke's performance was what counted. If LTC Smith gave a negative report about Luke to John, surely the probationary period would become much more difficult. This thought made Luke calm down and simply accept his fate for the time being.

"Also, sir: Agent Williams's reports focus on tunneling operations and signals intelligence-collection activities against the Soviets. I'd like to gain access to Project Groundhog."

"What is it you hope to gain from access to those operation files?" LTC Smith didn't quite know what to think about Luke's request. An investigation usually follows the facts to come to a conclusion, not the other way around. Luke's request sounded a lot like he was jumping to a conclusion and trying to find evidence to support his hypothesis.

"I think he may have been operationally involved during the time of the Soviets' discovery of the tunnel operations. If I know what he was reporting on, and the context of what he was doing with his sources for that project, as well as what the project's technology entailed, I may be able to better understand what personalities he may be working with, their motivation, training, and target of U.S. information, or even scientists they would target."

Smith allowed it to carry forward after Luke's explanation. He could oversee the investigation and use it as live-environment training, seeing as this was Luke's first real investigation outside the Schoolhouse. Although Luke seemed to be able to handle the investigation, he was on probation, as was any agent in their first year on the job. He had to be observed by a superior and report to a nonprobationary agent to ensure he was not breaking the law during an investigation, or take questions about processes to them for clarification. As an officer, LTC Smith had been trained on oversight of new agents but relied on John to clarify processes during an investigation. Still, LTC Smith had overseen a handful of probationary agents in the past and knew when to call an old head like John for help.

"Carry on, then, Luke. And good luck. Oh! And look into this 'girlfriend' Williams has. If she is pregnant with his kid, we need to know why that wasn't reported." Luke left LTC Smith's office with a renewed fervor for the case. Weeks of skulking around someone else's life can wear on a person, especially if it yields no results. Luke was ready to dive into the next step of the case: research and analytics. But he needed help.

Chapter 9

A Hot Cold War

Luke needed help with the next steps of the investigation. He knew LTC Smith would not allow for another agent to be reassigned, even temporarily, to help with this case. He had to leverage the assets around him.

"Sarah, think you can help out with the next step in the case?" Luke knew damn well she would jump at the chance. He didn't even stop long enough to get an answer from her. "I need all of Williams's files he made from fieldwork. I also need any reports, from anyone, regarding signal intelligence, tunnels, listening posts, hedgehog, groundhog, or worm, any of those topics should yield some results for the programs Williams was working on here in Bamberg or in Berlin. Don't worry about other locations in Europe; stick to those two locations in Germany."

Sarah nodded as she took notes. Then she stood from her chair and leaned closer to Luke, taking a quick look around to make sure no one was watching them. "Will you need me at night? Tonight? Or any other night this week? To help out with anything?" This is why Luke chose her as an assistant. Luke just smirked as he responded, "Maybe. Let's see how the rest of today goes before we arrange a meeting."

It took a week for Sarah to compile all the files she could get her hands on. They were all original, so some of them were a bit tricky to get out of the Records Section. The files went back ten years. The clerk wanted them returned in three weeks. Luke began the process by determining how much coffee he would need and where he could get a cot to keep in his office.

He knew this process would be painful. It took seven weeks, six days a week; 133 gallons of coffee; $200 in takeout from the Chinese food restaurant across the street from the walk-in gate of the Bamberg Complex; and two original Beatles albums to the Records Section clerk. That last one hurt Luke bad, as they were from his personal collection. Luke knew it would be worth it once he found the necessary evidence to catch Williams in the act of espionage.

Luke also had to find out who Williams's girlfriend was. He took a trip over to the German Liaison Office on the other side of the city. There were channels in place to obtain records on Americans. Usually the military police used this avenue to ensure American service members were paying off their parking tickets. Sometimes internal affairs came by to inquire about records for their use in investigations. Rarely intelligence agents came by to get information about Americans who expatriated for a variety of reasons. Because of the frequency and Status of Forces Agreements in place, little questions were asked, and records were simply handed over. Even though the United States was one of the victors over Nazi Germany, new governments were established on both sides of Germany. As a diplomatic courtesy, the Status of Forces Agreement, or S.O.F.A., allowed for information sharing or prosecution of errant service members by the appropriate government agency. Usually low-level crimes, such as public intoxication, were handled by the U.S. government, where capital charges, such as murder, were prosecuted by the local German government.

"I'm looking for marriage certificates for Americans in the last year," Luke stated to the clerk when he was summoned. The counterespionage badge he presented quietly next to the list of names caught the young lady's attention. "Just a standard security check, fraulein."

The young female clerk gave a quiet nod, took the list, and disappeared behind the counter. A moment later she popped back out. "Zis vill take a minuten, mein heir." Luke nodded and found a seat. After about twenty minutes, the young lady came out with a folder about two inches thick. "Zeez are the records ve have. Zey are the cover pages, not ze entire file. Vil you need more than zis?"

Luke looked a bit surprised at the sheer volume of American-German marriages in the last twelve months. These were *just* the cover sheets? Luke's amazement must have shown clearly on his face. The clerk offered an explanation.

"It vould zeem you Americans are very compatible vit our ladies. Or they are in a hurry to leave Deutschland." A look of intrigue came over her face as she looked at Luke. He figured she might be in a hurry to leave Germany too.

Luke thanked the young lady and made his way out of the office as quickly as he could. It was bad enough Sarah gave him that look, but he was in no hurry to put his clearance in jeopardy. With records in hand, he went back to the office.

Looking through the cover sheets, he wasn't optimistic he would find Williams's name in the pile but figured he may have taken the next step with the young lady. However, if Williams was spying, he might have run off and eloped with the young lady somewhere outside of American-German jurisdiction. As Luke systematically filed through the pages, he found it about halfway through. Williams had married Eva von Groussen. Williams was married to a foreign national and failed to report the information to the security department to update his records. To Luke, this was like knowing Al Capone was guilty of murder but having him arrested on tax evasion. While it was enough to take him down, there must be a bigger reason for not reporting the relationship. Luke wanted the big crime, not the small security violation; Williams's career could recover from this flub. He could say he didn't know he was supposed to report it or say he tried but no one cared. There were ways out for him.

In the meantime, Luke wanted to know more about von Groussen. The prefix "von" made him wonder if she was royalty or some other form of aristocrat. Luckily the local library had a robust German genealogy section. Searching through old family trees, microfiche, and Nazi documents from the war years, Luke was able to find the facts of von Groussen's family history. Luke doubted she knew as much about her own family history as he did. She wasn't royalty, but her paternal grandfather, Heimrich von Groussen, was an aristocrat. Heimrich was not very well connected politically, but he came from a wealthy land-owning family. That's where his title and money came from, not from his own efforts. The family was hit hard during the German economic crisis that followed World War I. Her grandfather, like many aristocratic Germans during that time, took kindly to the Nazis and increased the family's wealth before it was confiscated for the "betterment of all German peoples." Following World War II the family was disgraced and became farmers on a small plot of land owned for seven generations. It was the only real estate they had left from the policies of Hitler's Germany. Luke remembered the young clerk's words from earlier and wondered if Eva was the latter of the two categories of women.

But if she were trying to leave Germany, why would Williams stay there so long? What would compel him to stay there? Was he having too much fun? Was he going to stay there with her and raise a family? Did she want to leave? Would she not let him go? A feeling came over Luke. Did he really find a new piece of evidence or did he find just another bread crumb in Williams's espionage plot?

When he wasn't in the office, Luke had been living in the surveillance apartment. He made the front room look like someone lived there, but the bathroom and single bedroom were sparsely furnished. Sarah would come over on weekends and watch TV, play some old Beatles records, and have a drink every so often on the balcony, as to keep up appearances of a normal life inside the apartment. She didn't mind doing it, as it provided some semblance of a normal life her assigned barracks room lacked. Luke, meanwhile, had taken some time to identify someone who lived inside the building as a usable source.

"His name is Fritz, thirty-four years old, and he works as the building handyman. He expressed disdain for the Soviets and spoke about his parents' disdain for the Nazis. Other than that, he doesn't seem to have any political leanings," Luke explained to LTC Smith.

"And how much do you think it would take to get to get him to our side?" inquired Smith.

"Given his outlook on the Soviets, we may be able to convince him there are sympathizers living in the building. As far as payment goes, he has a good job, so just reimbursement of his time and any equipment he may have to procure. But if he needs to change a lock or fix a pipe, the building pays for those materials, so our overhead for source funding will be low."

"Go for it; recruit him for the purpose of identifying the woman, what her habits are, and who, if at all, she's working with."

Luke had to ensure Fritz would say yes to spy for the Americans. If he rushed into it, Fritz may go to the German government; if he was too aloof, Fritz may not know what he was talking about and the final drop of the curtain may show Luke's inexperience, or worse, incompetence.

It was a Friday night when Luke met Fritz for drinks in a small bar on the outskirts of the city. Luke kept pressing him for political affiliations to find out how susceptible Fritz would be to becoming a source. Fritz was vaguely aware of what Luke did for a living and what brought him to Germany. As the bar closed down and both were a little buzzed from the hefeweizen they were drinking, Luke invited Fritz back to the apartment for more drinks and to talk about life under postwar conditions. The front room had been scrubbed so no one would know it was being used for surveillance.

"Come on in, Fritz; make yourself comfortable." Luke wanted Fritz to be at ease when he presented the opportunity to help in the fight against the Soviets. "I think I woke my girlfriend up," Luke explained as Sarah began to stir about from the bedroom—all planned, of course.

"Late night, honey?" Sarah began, so as to keep the illusion alive for Fritz. "Did you see the news about the Russian tanks moving around in East Germany?"

"They are East German tanks, not Soviet," Fritz blurted out. He was well aware of current events as they pertained to his home possibly hosting another world war. "Those fucking bastards are tearing my country apart!"

It would appear recruiting Fritz may be easier than Luke thought. "Fritz, it sounds to me like you are an idealistic patriot," Luke started. "I just wonder if you're willing to do something to aid the fight."

Fritz suddenly looked sober as he placed his beer on the coffee table and leaned forward on the couch. "I think I know what this is about,"

Fritz said coyly. "You are more than just an American soldier, aren't you?"

Fritz was already aware of what was coming next, or so he thought. "We need your help to identify Soviet agents. Are you willing to help in that fight, Fritz?" Luke was blunt about the process instead of easing into his sales pitch.

"If it es information you is after, I am villing to help; as long as I do not have to go into harm's vey." Fritz was fully on board. The beer seemed to ease the idea of spying on people for him. "I am ready to help."

Luke explained how they would no longer be able to meet in public anymore, and the way they would communicate to each other would change drastically. Fritz was eager to aid in the fight and gave over everything he already knew. Luckily Luke had stocked the refrigerator with beer before he set out to meet Fritz at the bar.

"I zink there es someone in mein building who may be up to no good," he started without prompting. His eyes widened as he reached for his beer to tell the rest of the story. "There is an

American zoldier who frequents one of ze apartments of a German woman. They seem to sneak around, und she does not stay at the apartment often; one time a week, maybe."

Luke began to ask details of the American. After getting a description, he believed it was Williams. "There was an incident about two months ago ven de American showed up, running up the stairs frantically, und he dropped ein envelope. It looked like it came out of his jacket but was too big to fit inside of his coat pocket. He heard it drop, saw me in the hallway, und quickly turned to pick it up. He continued on his way to her apartment but continued to stare at me the whole time."

Luke continued to debrief Fritz. The more he laid out the details, the more Luke was sure Williams was passing information. Luke now had enough to ask for further investigative action.

As Luke showed Fritz out of the apartment, Sarah came around the corner from the kitchen. "Are you going to take this to LTC Smith?"

Convinced Luke may take his own initiative instead of asking for permission, Sarah made her inquiry to help Luke with his decision on how and when to talk to LTC Smith.

"I need to go out and think about all this. Stay here, won't you?" Luke asked, but he was really ordering. Several hours later Luke came back smelling like whiskey, but he seemed to have all his faculties.

"We need to find out what projects Williams has been working on," Luke stated while looking down at the ground. Sarah was trying to make sense of what he was saying in her tired stupor. It was about four in the morning at this point. "And I'll need further authorization from LTC Smith."

Sarah sighed her relief audibly as her shoulders went limp. It was as if a weight had been lifted off her. "Now that you have settled this issue, please come to bed. Some of us have to work in the morning," Sarah said as a joke. Luke just stared at the carpeted floor of the apartment, lost in thought.

The next day Luke went to LTC Smith to inform him of his intentions. When he approached the door, it was shut and he could hear a conversation taking place. He knocked anyway and was summoned in almost immediately. To his delight, John was there.

"Oh, hello, sir!" Luke said before looking at LTC Smith. "LTC Smith, good morning. How are you, sir? Is everything all right?"

"John was just in town for business and we were discussing the particulars of your case. I hope you don't mind his input to any further guidance." LTC Smith appeared to give the option, but it was really an order; the case would be shared with John.

"That's what I came to talk to you about, sir. I believe Williams has been sharing information with a young lady." Luke handed a file across the desk as he shut the door. Inside were his notes from debriefing Fritz, memorandums to document his actions through the case, and a diagram showing timeframes and venues frequented by Williams.

After Smith looked over the information, he handed it over to John for his intake of the situation. "It looks like a thorough investigation is under way. What do you think, John?"

"It depends on what Luke thinks the next move is, sir." John placed the burden on the young agent to articulate why he should have access to programs and files he was not a part of. John was still testing Luke.

"Well, sir, I think he may be handing off information dealing with signals intelligence, as that is what Williams has access to daily." Luke made this suggestion hoping LTC Smith would read his mind and answer with authorization to the current program files. "I would have to look at the files to understand what is currently going on to develop a list of possible intelligence targets." LTC Smith still wasn't biting. "May I have access to those files, sir?" Luke finally asked directly.

LTC Smith and John looked at each other a little puzzled. LTC Smith began to question Luke to shed light on their confusion. "Your notes are many and incoherent. What is it your source told you?"

"Give the bullet points, facts, not opinion, on what they told you," John chimed in to clarify LTC Smith's question. Luke complied and orally laid out his notes from what his meeting with Fritz had revealed. After Luke finished, LTC Smith and John each exhaled heavily before making eye contact. John nodded his head toward LTC Smith. "Please, after you."

"I think the next step is to see if Williams is actually taking anything from the vault. Before jumping to the conclusion and finding evidence to support, agents must follow the trail. We think he is handing off information obtained in hard copy, which would explain the folder your source said he dropped in the stairwell," John offered in opinion. LTC Smith agreed.

"So now you need to find someone in Williams's section who has daily interaction with him but is not so close as to feel obligated to report your investigation to him," John continued. "Then we, or rather you, can find out if he has other flags for possibly committing espionage."

Luke smirked. "I think I already have someone in mind, sir. Her name is Sarah, and she has access to the vault. I enlisted her help for collating and filing papers as well as providing cover for me to appear out and about town, like a normal couple."

"Well, thanks for asking me, Luke," LTC Smith retorted. Luke figured it was easier to ask forgiveness than permission. "I hope that's all you are doing as a couple, Luke," LTC Smith stated. "We don't need this whole thing falling apart because of a jilted lover."

Luke assured both men he was not engaged in more than anything completely professional with her. "She's been a great asset to the investigation, and now she can aid in further steps and analytics."

"Sounds good to me. John?" LTC Smith said, asking for guidance from an experienced voice. John nodded his head in approval. "It's settled, then. I'll have her reassigned from the vault.

Williams has been asking for an analyst, so he gets his wish, and she can act as your source on Williams's work habits."

Chapter 10

Smoke and Mirrors

After two weeks of being reassigned to work in the vault, Sarah met with Luke at the safe house. She couldn't wait to tell him what she had found. She ran up the stairs, skipping steps, and flung the door open, giving Luke quite the scare. "He's been falsifying reports, Luke," Sarah let out before trying to catch her breath. "I heard the Russians talk about movement, but the report that came out stated they were going to leave their troops in place," Sarah blurted out wildly.

"Calm down, Sarah" Luke said in an angry tone as he rubbed the sides of his head. "Start from the beginning and tell me where you were, dates of occurrences, how you heard it, and where those transcripts went," Luke said calmly before turning to get her a glass of water.

"It was on Thursday, when I was asked to sit in the vault where they have the tapes come in from the tunnel, like I told you about last week. We play them back and an interpreter translates what they are saying as they speak. I was there to take notes and Williams was asking follow-up questions to determine what was said versus what was meant."

"Were the Russians speaking plainly? That is to say, did the interpreter state they were planning on moving troops? Personnel? Soldiers?" Luke asked sharply as he raised his hands in the air to emphasize the need for Sarah to tell him verbatim what the interpreter said.

"No, they referred to 'ants' making home closer to the wall. They tried to be cryptic with their conversation. But it went on like that—ants and walls and tubes and dragons..."

"Hold on, hold on. What do you think they meant by tubes and dragons?" Luke asked.

"I think they know about the signal intelligence tunnel we have. And the way they were talking about ants and dragons near the wall made me think they were referring to tanks." Sarah was wringing her forehead as she described the situation.

Luke pressed Sarah to go on with the events. She described in detail how she and the interpreter thought the Russians were describing troop movements toward the Berlin Wall and the possibility they found the tunnel. Luke did everything he could to separate hypothesis from fact.

"Williams kept telling us to calm down and put the seed of doubt into us. He kept saying we were coming to conclusions without facts and we needed to report only the facts." Sarah collapsed onto the couch and continued to drink the water Luke brought her. "He said they didn't know about the tunnel and we had to keep operations going to continue the fight. And then this morning I saw a requisition going to LTC Smith asking for more personnel and new equipment to go toward the tunnel operation."

Luke knew what Sarah meant when she described Williams getting them to collect facts and not jump to conclusions. He was right, but they still needed to discuss the possibility of the Russians moving troops and tanks. Talk in the vault was just that: talk. But what needed to get reported was fact, as told by the field agents in their reports.

"Let's go back one step: Last week you said it was your job to collect and file all the reports. What happened to these reports about ants and dragons?" Luke inquired.

"Williams took them and said he would file them. But he doesn't normally do that. He always leaves that to lower enlisted personnel," Sarah said in a defeated state. Now Luke knew why she was in such a tizzy. "The file was on his desk when we left for lunch and gone when we came back."

Asking the obvious, Luke inquired, "Well, did he file them in the right place?"

"I looked in the file storage rack and the files were a photocopy."

"How did you know it was a photocopy?"

"We write analysts' notes on the originals, and the file present didn't have the indentation from my pen. It was photocopied," Sarah said.

"Williams filed the report, which he doesn't usually do. He didn't file them immediately, and when he finally did, they were photocopies. Are photocopies not allowed?" Luke usually had Sarah to take care of filing, so it didn't seem odd to have photocopies.

"Photocopies of a file have to be signed off on by LTC Smith. The authorization to do so would have been filed in the back of the original copies. And there is one person responsible for making the copies, and their signature is required on the sheet as well. That document was not in the file."

Luke ran through the plausible reasons for there being a photocopy: Maybe Williams forgot the sheet. Maybe the photocopy personnel were in on the whole affair with Williams. Maybe this was just sloppy security practices. Even with those explanations, Luke still had enough circumstantial evidence to go to LTC Smith for more authorizations into the investigation. He could get technicians to bug the apartment; he could search Williams's mail; he could even begin bringing in others from around the office for interviews. Luke poured Sarah a glass of scotch, let her sip and unwind from the past day's events, and began writing his report.

The next day, Luke went into the office to hand the report to LTC Smith personally. Luke didn't make it ten feet inside the building when he realized something big was going on. As he got closer to his office, he could hear the phone ringing. Luke rushed in to answer. "Luke, it's LTC Smith. I'm calling in all agents. We need accountability of everyone and their assets. Get into the office now."

Luke hurried down the hallway to LTC Smith's office and saw another agent leaving. He looked rough and had files in hand marked "Secret/No Foreign." It looked like a source dossier. LTC Smith saw Luke approaching and waved him in. As Luke entered, there were stacks of files and Smith looked pissed.

"Close the door," LTC Smith ordered. Luke complied and sat down. "A source was killed in East Berlin last night. It's a message from the Russians."

"How do we know it's not an accident or robbery gone wrong?" Luke offered as plausible explanations.

"They hung his body from a building in plain sight of Checkpoint Charlie. Their tanks are on the move." LTC Smith was chain-smoking and flipping through files while he talked. "What is your take on Williams? Could he have leaked out the information on a source?" Luke was suddenly scared. He didn't know why, but he was suddenly overtaken and started to wonder if there was something he had done wrong in his investigation. "You're the only one leading an investigation on anyone right now; I need to know if this was Williams's work."

Luke handed over the report regarding the photocopied reports. LTC Smith dropped the report and leaned forward onto his desk. "And when the hell did you get this information, Luke?"

"Last night, sir. I typed it up and was going to give it to you today." Luke had sunk in his chair when Smith began his questioning. "I didn't see any imminent dangers, so I followed protocol in the seventy-two-hour reporting requirement. I thought we had more time to act on this."

"Well, we need to make a move now. I'll get the judge advocate general on the phone and see what our next step is, legally speaking. I don't want to be paranoid, but we can't afford to let a suspected espionage agent run free."

Things began to move fast after the source was killed. The JAG signed off on a search warrant of Williams's off-post apartment, his car, and his office. They arranged for the military police to apprehend him, as he didn't show up to work that morning. Luke and Smith questioned the absence as a sign of guilt. Did he leave? Defect to Soviet controlled territory? Or worse?

"I'll head over to Williams's apartment, sir," Luke informed LTC Smith. As Luke turned to walk out of the office, LTC Smith called to him.

"No! Let the military police handle this, Luke. We have no idea what state of mind Williams might be in. Let the guys with guns handle bringing him in."

In another part of the city, ,military police Jeeps raced through the centuries-old streets, sirens blaring, in an effort to reach Williams's apartment before he left. Given the timeframe of events, either Williams would have been there or he would have fled hours prior. When the military police showed up to Williams's apartment, they found his wife pounding on the bedroom door, sobbing. They knew he was still there. The question was, what situation lay behind the door?

Smoke and Mirrors | 167

"Please tell me what is happening, Mitch. Why are you leaving? What are these men doing here? What kind of trouble are you in? Please, please... talk to me! What is happening?" After prying her away from the door, the military police kicked it in. They found Williams sitting on the bed, slumped over; he was drunk and crying. "I'm ready to talk," Williams stated without prompting. As one military policeman loaded him into a patrol Jeep, another held his wife at bay.

"Where are you taking him? What has he done?" she asked frantically as she held her pregnant belly. The police wouldn't tell her what was going on, but the look on her face clearly showed she knew Williams wouldn't be there to raise their child.

Luke desperately wanted to be there when the military police arrested Williams but knew he had to stay away. A situation like that could become very dangerous for Luke; it was best if the guys with guns did what they were trained to do. Luke would only get in the way. He desperately wanted to talk to Williams's wife, but the rules of which agents could interrogate her were clear. She was left for the German police to interview.

Williams was taken to the police station on post while his apartment was searched. Not like it needed to be. There were four shoeboxes filled with U.S. currency on his bed and a pistol, unloaded, next to them. He knew the game was over. In a defeated state, he had packed up all the evidence so his wife wouldn't have to be subjected to the house being pulled apart. Even with all the effort he put into preparation for a search, the investigators and military police tore everything apart anyway. Maybe it was because they didn't care about the feelings of a traitor, or maybe it was just in their nature when going after a perp. Either way, insult was added to injury.

Luke met Williams at the police holding cell. "Would you mind if I talk to him alone?" Luke asked. "I just want to soften him up before the interview." The military policemen looked at each other apprehensively, knowing full well there should be someone present if Williams should incriminate himself. But for whatever reason, they felt comfortable with Luke and allowed him to pull up a seat next to the steel bars separating the two.

"Before anything else, I need to know who else may be in danger," Luke started. Williams lay on his cell bed, silent. Luke could smell the whiskey coming out of Williams's pores. He must have been drinking since the night prior to have that much in him. He must have known about the source's murder, or taken part in it.

"Judging by the way your wife reacted to the military police showing up, I can't imagine she was in on the plot. At least, from the way the officers tell the story." Williams said nothing. He just stared off into the corner. "What I don't understand is, if she wasn't committing espionage with you, why keep her a secret? Did you marry her to throw us off our tracks? Was she cover for... something else in your life? You don't seem to be very popular with the ladies, as folks in your office describe you." Williams wiped a tear away from his eye as he shifted his eyes down to the floor of the cell. "Can I get you a coffee? It may help sober you up."

"You knew what this was. You knew it could have been stopped," Williams retorted. "The signs were there and you did nothing. No one was supposed to get hurt. Spies don't hang anymore, Luke. We get put on public trial before being condemned to rot in a cell until need for a swap. I believe in the cause. I believe in a just society. But I know what life is like behind the Iron Curtain. I can't live in America anymore, and Soviets won't trust me if I defect. Or defected. I guess that option is off the table now."

"I'll get you that coffee," Luke said quietly as he rose from his seat. Luke looked out of the holding area to ensure the military police could not hear their conversation. He walked to the corner of the holding area where a stationery and coffee station was set up. Among the paperwork and first-aid supplies was the state-of-the-art coffee bar to help the night crews stay awake, and to sober up soldiers thrown into the drunk tank.

"How will history judge us?" Williams asked. "Will we be seen as patriots?" Luke stopped with his back to Williams but did not respond. "Will we be seen as having picked a side when the sides were unclear; or were the distinctions black and white?"

"The facts will show where you stand in history," Luke said as he poured black coffee into two paper cups, one of them for himself. "What else does the woman in the apartment you met at know about your operations?" Luke began.

"You're just looking for some insurance in the whole matter, aren't you?" Williams slurred out while reaching for the coffee. "You're gonna have to wait and find out."

There was no need to continue talking to Williams. Anything he was going to say would be said through the course of interviews. Luke understood what Williams's intentions were.

As Luke was signing out of the police station front desk, several military policemen were running into the holding cell area. One called out to get a medic. In all the searching for evidence, it seems Williams himself was not searched. The cyanide capsule he had concealed was overlooked. Luke finished the coffee he had poured for himself and walked out of the police station still holding on to the paper cup.

Chapter 11

John's Investigation

The day after Luke's disappearance, John found himself in LTC Smith's office. "Any indication on where Luke may be going, John?" John sat silently. As a counterespionage agent, he should have known the signs. He should have figured something was wrong when the Russians freed Luke from captivity so quickly. He should have questioned why Luke had pushed for additional training beyond his skills and experience.

"Who, if anyone, was Luke meeting with? What was his relationship to Sarah?" John wondered out loud. "I'd like to see Williams's source dossier, sir. If we can figure out who he was meeting with, and any overlap between him and Luke, we may be able to piece this thing together."

LTC Smith pointed to a banker's box in the corner. A piece of red tape covered the outside with the word "Evidence" on it. LTC Smith knew this was coming and ordered the file be brought in for John to assess. John was given permission to start the investigation, although LTC Smith thought he might be too emotionally invested in the whole affair.

"I'll be in town for a couple weeks to look into the matter," John said, emotionless.

"John?" started LTC Smith. "We've known each other for fifteen years now. I don't know that I've ever seen any events hit so close to home for you."

"Is there a question in there, Jacob?" John asked accusingly to LTC Smith.

"Are you sure you can handle this investigation? Are you going to be able to divorce your emotions from what's happened here?"

"And what happened here? No one knows. An investigation needs to be undertaken. If it would make you feel better, I'll keep you informed, and if anything too personal is uncovered, I'll hand the case off to another agent." Inside John desperately wanted to scream at LTC Smith to stay out of his way, but that would just give Smith more reason to recommend John not be assigned to the case.

"Sounds fair, John. Sounds fair." LTC Smith gave what he thought was a smile, but to John it looked like the same face someone gets when they tell a hospitalized friend they look good. It wasn't very reassuring to John. But he went about with the investigation, anyway.

John walked over to Luke's office to rummage around. A cursory look may reveal some reason why Luke had left. As John opened the door to Luke's office, he knew he wouldn't find anything of value. The desk was neat and clean, ready to take on the next case. The drawers were empty; John even found dust in them, like they hadn't been touched in months. The tops of the filing cabinets were dust-free, the floor swept and mopped, and the trash can was empty. There wasn't even a new bag in it. John closed the door; Luke's office was best to look at later.

John's thoughts ran back to cases he had handled in the past. Iran, 1968 Democratic National Convention, Vietnam—they were all against the adversary selling secrets from outside his office. No one inside the circle of trusted agents had done this during his career. Other agencies had their problems, and other countries too. But an espionage agent within his own ranks was new territory for him. Willy would have to find a new job; that much was certain. Even though John, Mike, and Dave were working with Luke the most, they weren't in charge. For how disheartened John felt about the whole affair, he was thankful he had turned down leadership positions; and this was why. If you were there and it happened, it was your fault.

John tried to shake those thoughts and focus on the case. John figured Sarah might know what was going on. John had LTC Smith call the military police from his office to coordinate keeping an eye on her until morning. "We don't know where she is. They checked her barracks room, but it only had some field gear in the wall locker. It's like she took her personal effects and took off. Do you think she was in on it too, John?" John could hear in LTC Smith's voice he was awaiting a similar fate of Willy. If punishment came through, he might be able to retire instead of simply being dishonorably discharged.

"I don't know. Does she have any friends she stays with? Has she ever talked about a favorite destination around town?" John wanted to wait until morning to get a running start at this case, but he was going to have to work through the night to get some facts together before he made a phone call to higher-ups. They would not be pleased to find out another soldier was in on the operation. John glanced over in the corner of LTC Smith's office and noticed a cot and some blankets being held down by a pillow. It looked like LTC Smith was planning on living in the office until this issue was resolved.

"I don't think she associated with anyone outside the office, other than on German Fridays. And with Luke."

"Was Luke assigned a barracks room?" John had nothing to go on and started fishing for answers.

"He lived off post. From time to time he stayed at the apartment we rented for surveillance operations, I think."

"That's where we need to go. Both locations. Get the military police to head to each location. I'll go to the surveillance site; you go to his apartment." LTC Smith must have come to the same conclusion; he was picking up the phone before John could finish his statement.

A quick phone call later they were out the door. John got the address from LTC Smith as they walked out the front door of the building and headed to their respective cars to meet the military police at each location. John got to the surveillance apartment before the police arrived. He cautiously made his way up the stairs and counted the numbers on the doors as he got closer to the address.

When he arrived, he thought twice about trying to go in but was too excited, angry, and curious to stay in the hallway. He slowly turned the doorknob until he realized it was unlocked. He thought about the scenarios that could be awaiting him on the other side but took the risk anyway. He drew a pistol from his jacket and laid his shoulder into the door, swinging it wildly open. There was Sarah on the couch, crying.

"He's not coming back, is he?" she asked. Though she didn't know who John was, she knew what he was there for. John didn't answer her. He just put the pistol away and sat down next to her.

"We don't know where he is. You can help us, Sarah." He went into a sales pitch to get her to cooperate. "Luke deceived a lot of people. He took advantage of you, Sarah. If you want to help Luke, then please help us. We don't know why he left, or what he's out there doing."

Sarah nodded her head. She wanted to see Luke again so badly she was willing to tell John everything she knew. John knew Luke as this tenderfoot with a certain uncertainty about who he was. But from what Sarah detailed, he was a brilliant young man with all the answers. He was meticulous about not talking about his upbringing, where he was from, what he did before he arrived at Bamberg, or what had happened on the doomed mission.

Over the next week, Luke's office was searched, his apartment was searched, and the surveillance site was searched. There was nothing found. There wasn't even a trace of Fritz having been there: no hairs, fingerprints, or fibers were found. They only found a couple of Sarah and John's hairs on the couch from the night Luke disappeared. The only files left in Luke's office were the ones originally in the office when he was first assigned there.

John moved on to the banker's box LTC Smith had given him. He didn't think he would find much to aid in tracking down Luke but figured it may help shed some light on what happened. He stared at the box with despair. He didn't want to open it. He wanted to let the case go and hope Luke turned up the victim of the Soviets. But he still wanted closure. He pulled back the red tape labeled "Evidence" and removed the lid.

Inside he found the source dossier for the Baker. John thought it funny the source would have the same code name as one of his former assets. Then he saw the smoking gun:

Source Real Name: Ingrid

Former U.S. Involvement: East Berlin Safe House Keeper

Current U.S. Involvement: None

Reason for Termination: Termination without Prejudice; Operation terminated 04/1984 due to compromise of field agent and secondary source.

The code name was no coincidence; the Baker had been terminated from U.S. operations and left East Berlin. As an intermediary for U.S. agents crossing through the checkpoint, she was privileged to snippets of information. It was apparent she gave up information pertaining to Luke and the Mechanic. But why would Luke leave? What was he hiding? Did he figure it out as well and went rogue to enact revenge for getting turned over to suffer at the hands of the Russian major?

Through his investigation, John had determined Williams had been meeting with the Baker in the apartment under surveillance by Luke. According to the files, Williams was not reporting his activities with her. She wasn't getting paid by him, she wasn't being run as an asset or source by him, nor was she giving assistance to U.S. mission, either. So what were they meeting for?

Playing devil's advocate, John had to ask about the possibility of Luke having been in on the plot. What if the cyanide capsule that killed

Williams was not taken by his own hand? What if Luke had given it to him? John didn't want to think someone under his guidance could have been a spy without his knowing it, but that was the very nature of spying—committing espionage without anyone knowing it.

If Luke had been keeping accurate surveillance notes, there would be no way he or any agent would fail to identify Ingrid, even if it was just an in-depth description and pattern of life: where she went, when she left the apartment, what her activities outside the apartment were, and others she would meet with, even if it was just in passing.

John pulled all of Luke's files to pore over notes and reports. There had to be additional files he had put into records about the investigation. If Luke had them, clues could be found as to the accuracy and diligence of Luke's efforts. And if there were none, John could theorize Luke was in on the nefarious activities.

John called down to place a request to the Records Section. The clerk informed him all the records had been requested by LTC Smith already. Whatever had been in the vault had been boxed up and sent to LTC Smith's office in a banker's box with red tape labeled "Evidence" on it. While this revelation was no smoking gun, it was enough to justify John's next move.

"I need a personnel roster of all human resources personnel assigned to the Bamberg G1 section for the past seven months," John told LTC Smith.

"Where is your investigation taking you, John?" LTC Smith inquired.

"If Luke had been involved with Williams's actions, he would have needed someone to get him assigned here with him. Someone would have had the ability to pull those strings to get him assigned here specifically." It made sense. The G1 handled all personnel actions—awards, leave, and assignments. One particular action that took place in the G1 was identifying who had what skills to fill assignments. Generals rarely, if ever, reviewed this information. They simply took the G1's word those candidates were the best for the job.

"Do you think there may still be another mole within the command?" LTC Smith was already fearful for his career, but John's theory made him believe this would be the final nail in the coffin.

"I can at least suspect there is." John had his hands on his hips and looked down at the floor of LTC Smith's office as he quietly confirmed his suspicions. "I need to interview all of those personnel to see what they know."

"I'll make the appropriate arrangements, John," LTC Smith said as he lit a cigarette. The next day he and John worked on scheduling all of the identified personnel from the G1 who were assigned to Bamberg during the timeframe Luke was taken prisoner and subsequently released. There were four still remaining.

"Should we notify Army G1 to track the others, John?" LTC Smith was on the right track but didn't know the investigative steps like John.

"Let's interview these four first, then, if needed, we can have other field offices reach out to the others if they are still in service. For any who may have left the military, we can leverage the Federal Bureau of Investigation to track them down; I have a connection I can reach out to so we can keep this relatively quiet." John didn't want to make that call but would if needed. He hadn't spoken to Agent Johnston since his days on the COINTELPRO team in Chicago.

It was Tuesday when John and LTC Smith had their first of four remaining G1 personnel. After several hours of interview, John was well aware of how the personnel selection process worked but nothing about how Luke was assigned. He gained even less from the second interview. But the third G1 soldier interviewed was very helpful. She was the one who had recommended Luke be assigned to Bamberg in the first place.

"I thought Williams was just trying to get a good agent assigned. He said Luke went to the Schoolhouse with him. He told me what happened to Luke and how he was too valuable to lose. America needed Luke to oversee the cases Williams had been working on." While her speech was calm, she had tears streaming down her cheeks. "I didn't realize until all this happened I had taken part in it."

John had his answer. Luke and Williams had been working together. How did they go to the schoolhouse together? They attended training years apart. So why did Williams recommend Luke? But to what extent? Were they both working with Ingrid? Was Luke really taken by the Soviets, or did he give himself up to them? Did Luke give up NT? Was he responsible for the compromise of all the guys at the office? The evidence found by John's investigation left more questions than answers, and eventually the case went cold.

Chapter 12

Closure

Seven years had passed, and the treachery of Luke had been forgotten by most. It was the questions left behind that haunted the intelligence professionals who partook in the ensuing investigation. His actions were taught in the Schoolhouse as an example of how to screen future agents in an attempt to prevent it from happening again, but the names and places were changed slightly to spare any embarrassment to the intelligence community as a whole. John's superiors didn't want his reputation tarnished but needed to cite the lessons learned as a cautionary tale of what not to do.

Meanwhile John was reassigned to Paris to oversee an office dedicated to aiding in the stabilization of Europe after the Berlin Wall came down. He was now in a full-time managerial position and didn't leave to conduct fieldwork anymore—his penance for not having caught Luke before he did his damage. From time to time John would liaison with the French police or internal security services. It was a part of fieldwork but more of an ancillary administrative task he personally undertook. Others who knew of what transpired suspected he was still searching for Luke, maybe in the hopes of regaining his good name in the counterespionage community.

It was during one of these routine meetings with the Parisian District Security liaison that brought Luke back into John's life. "And you're saying he's here? Living here?"

"Oui. He has been coming to Paris under different names for the last two years." The security officer took a sip of his coffee before continuing. "We do not take actions against our partners' affairs," the liaison said, sliding a piece of paper to John. "This is credible information for you and your government to take action on as you see fit. We only ask you keep things quiet. We enjoy a partnership through diplomatic relations and do not want to have to take adverse action against you and your department."

"Who else knows this information? Who outside your branch knows of his whereabouts?" John inquired with a raised eyebrow as he tipped his sunglasses down his nose. The answer was no one.

That evening as the sun was setting, John made his way down a main street and turned into the winding alleys leading to where Luke had rented a small apartment. The area was tucked away from the glamorous tourist attractions of the City of Lights. The location was a bit dirty for Parisian standards, but it also allowed for limited foot traffic and only had one way in or out. John knocked on the door as he would any other, but inside his heart was pounding. He certainly hoped the information was still good. He knew what he wanted to do if Luke opened the door, but he also knew what he should do.

As Luke opened the door, he looked relieved. It seemed as if his days of running were over. "Would you like a cup of coffee, John?" Luke offered as if he were greeting an old friend instead of the man who would bring justice in whatever form that was. John didn't say a word and entered the apartment.

An awkward silence hung in the air as Luke prepared two coffees. "I suppose you have some questions for me before you take me to the embassy."

"As you could imagine, I was a part of the investigative team following your disappearance. I know you had a surveillance station set up opposite Ingrid's apartment. At what point did you know it was her? When did you find out?" John wanted answers from Luke to understand the case better, not like it mattered much at this point.

"The order from Moscow came down months before I was assigned to Berlin. Williams was sloppy with his work. He was careless with how he handled taking information and covering his tracks. He could have made copies for his own use, for example, instead of putting the copies back in the vault. He could have focused on the mission instead of being corrupt and living a double and triple life. He said he was sympathetic to the cause but kept asking for more money. He associated with loose women and enjoyed his time in Germany. In some ways he was a typical American service member. In others he was extraordinarily greedy, and that led to him being sloppy. He was easy to catch, and he would have compromised the entire operation. He had to be taken out, and it needed to look like it was his fault."

Luke handed John a cup of coffee. John looked intently into the cup with some hesitation and placed the cup on the table.

"Did you slip him the cyanide capsule?" John asked.

"I didn't think he would take it willingly. After the conversation he and I had in Ingrid's apartment, it was evident he was going to turn himself in as soon as he gathered enough evidence on me." Luke took a sip of his coffee. "I bet this changes your questioning now, doesn't it?"

"And how often were you meeting with Williams?" John had entered interrogation mode. He wanted to know everything he could before he wasn't able to talk to Luke. His reputation had been called into question after Luke had been taken by the Soviets during the East Berlin mission. The twilight years of an illustrious career had become an anecdote for lessons learned in the Schoolhouse—lessons in what not to do.

"As soon as I confirmed Williams was the agent, I was sent in and cornered him. I tried to talk some sense into him to return to the task at hand for the Motherland. He seemed reluctant to turn away from capitalism. He said he wanted equality for all peoples but continued to seek more money and... things: cars, apartments, trips around Europe. These things mean nothing when there are injustices in the world that Communism provides a cure for."

"The only thing I want to know is why. What was so repulsive about the United States you felt it necessary to betray it?" John asked accusingly.

"It was the ideals we as Americans stand for. It was the ideology of fighting for something that had nothing to do with us. Stripping people of their dignity and choices to be free of the bourgeoisie class. It was the ideas that allowed the subjugation of the proletariat. The United States preaches equality for all but then turns around and imposes different laws for those under the poverty line. There should be no reason this inequality exists. There was no reason for Vietnam; there was no reason to exert so much power across the world when no one asked for it."

"But that's not your decision to make, Luke," John stated quietly. The anger was boiling inside him, but he knew Luke was caught. That thought kept him calm. "When did you—with a graduate degree, good upbringing, hell, running water and plenty of food in the grocery stores—decide things were unfair? And unfair to whom, Luke? What made you think things were so bad you had to contribute to the downfall of your nation? How did you feel left out in the dark with a system, as you say, that discriminates against minorities?"

"I felt the best way to contribute to history was to be a part of it, not to observe it."

"And when did this feeling start?" John asked. He needed to know the circumstances of Luke being flipped to the opposition. "What did the Russians do to you in captivity that made you think this way?"

"It was well before that, John. My parents knew their counterculture revolution could only do so much. When my parents heard the news about their fellow Weather Underground activist dying by their own homemade bomb, they knew violence was not an effective tool. They knew political dissidence was what would change the world. I sought out the right people in college to help me effect that change," Luke explained. "I knew there were other Americans who felt the same way, and I felt it was my duty to work toward the good of the cause, to see equality for all peoples. When the Society for an Equal America told me about their organization and the good they were doing, I chose to be a part of it. They were doing more by actually committing to the ideals, not just protesting and making newspapers. The Society, as we called it, had the active front using the First Amendment to protest policies and injustices in Western society. It was their KGB-funded wing that interested me. They worked with those in the Illegals Program; they looked like Americans, acted, spoke, spent money, all like Americans. But they were taking part in a clandestine collection program. They were the ones who convinced me to join the Company and do some real damage; they knew I had enough question marks in my background to appear legitimate. The order to work on these operations came from Moscow well before Berlin, John."

"When you say the order came down from Moscow before Berlin, are you telling me the order came directly to you? Were you in contact, direct contact, with the KGB before we hired you? Was East Berlin even an accident, Luke?" John asked quietly.

"Ingrid and I had been told about each other well in advance. How do you think I was assigned to your unit before being trained and vetted properly? This is a big operation. Was, anyway," Luke said as he looked down, knowing the war had been lost. The symbol of his ideology's defense had been torn down and the world waited to see how the dissolution of the Soviet Union would play out.

"So the Russian major, he was part of the plan as well, I take it?" John stood up and took a step toward Luke as if he wanted to hit him. When Luke was taken by the Russians on that fateful mission, the team was thrown into a full panic mode; reports had to go up, John was in a marathon of briefings to commanders, and a plan had to be laid out to attempt to find his location and launch a rescue mission. The president and ambassadors had to be briefed on the possibility of another shooting war in Europe should the rescue operation kill Russian military or KGB officers. John was almost fired due to the failure of the simple snatch-and-run mission Luke was sent on.

"The Russian major didn't know who I was until... not until my Moscow contact, the KGB agent who handled me, came in and explained to the major. I'm sorry for all the trouble you and the guys had to go through, but it was necessary."

In a soft but accusatory tone, John asked, "Necessary for what, Luke? To ultimately lose the Cold War?"

"History will show what we did to stand up for our beliefs against the tyranny of the West," Luke said without confidence. He no longer looked John in the eyes when he spoke. Luke slowly took a seat at the small table in the corner, bringing his coffee in close to his chest.

"And how much of history will remember you, Luke? You're a traitor to the winning side.

Look out there; the Wall has fallen. You lost," John said simply, with a hint of smugness.

"Maybe we lost the battle, but the war is just beginning. The United States has now created a vacuum for the next dictator to take hold. It may not be in Europe or Asia. It could be Africa or South America. You can't fight a war against an idea, John."

"I hope you can live with the consequences of your actions, Luke."

"I hope you can live with yours, John."

John picked up the lukewarm cup of coffee off the table and left the apartment with it; he left the front door open. A man with a black suit entered and drew a pistol from his coat. This wasn't the closure John was hoping to get from a life's work fighting for his nation, but it was necessary, nonetheless.

Although the pistol had a silencer on it, John could still hear the action of the slide, a groan, and the muffled thud of a body hitting the floor as he made his way into the alley. He threw the coffee onto the street and loosely held the handle with one finger. He didn't even notice the partially dissolved casing of the cyanide capsule; he didn't need to. This was the last battle he had to fight against the tyranny of Communism. With no more loose ends to take care of, it was time for John to retire.